WHEN CARY MET THE GOOD GUYS

A CARY REDMOND SHORT STORY ANTHOLOGY

KAT SIMONS

Published 2020 by T&D Publishing
Cover design: © 2020 Evernight Designs
Interior book design © 2020 T&D Publishing
ISBN-13: 978-1-944600-30-3 (Trade Paperback Edition)

First printing T&D Publishing edition: December 2020
For information, contact T&D Publishing: https://tanddpublishing.com

See how it all got started.

Cary Redmond is just an ordinary woman contemplating a new career when she gets "tricked" into the life of a magical Protector. A paying job, which is always good, but still, not exactly something she'd trained for.

Her first year's introduction to magic and mystery proves eventful, and not always in a good way. But as Cary learns to survive her new job, she meets some of the most important people (and pets!) in her life.

These are their stories…

For good friends and beloved pets both current and past.

CONTENTS

WHEN CARY MET JAXER

When Cary met Jaxer, her life changed forever. Not that she wasn't already looking for a change. But still. Rethinking her career goals was one thing. Finding out the world was a lot spookier than she knew, quite another.

Cary never intended to jump head first into that strange, new world. But for a soft hearted animal lover, there were just some things she couldn't allow. And seeing a poor little Labrador puppy taking abuse from a huge man pushed her beyond her tolerance…right into one of the scariest moments of her life.

And the beginnings of a new adventure she may not survive.

See how it all began. When Cary Met Jaxer.

1

Cary Redmond reconsidered her life plans as she wandered out of the movie theater, leaving behind the yummy scent of popcorn to take the long route along NW Glisan St back to her apartment. Wondering if she had what it took, if she could do all the things she'd have to do in her chosen profession.

The Portland night air was crisp and cold, an earlier rain leaving the sidewalk wet. Streetlamps cast secure little patches of light as she walked past businesses mostly closed for the night and houses and apartment buildings lit with occupants. Christmas decorations bejeweled the occasional balcony or front yard. A huge menorah sat at the ready outside the Beth Israel temple, awaiting the first night of Hanukah.

She pulled her wool coat tighter around her as a cold breeze kicked up. She usually loved this time of year. All the holidays and gifts and lights and family events. But this year, this month, she was having a hard time getting into the spirit of things.

Being a veterinary technician wasn't all about helping save precious pet lives. She'd known that going in, but the reality was a lot harder than she'd anticipated. She'd had to help put someone's beloved pet dog to sleep that morning, and she really hated that part of the job.

It had been the right decision for the poor dog. Gallup was old and cancer riddled. It was time for him to rest.

But the anguished tears of Gallup's owner when the old terrier had stopped breathing had broken Cary's heart. She kept tearing up every time she thought about Glenda's sobs. She could still hear the sound.

Could she do that for the rest of her life?

That question had driven her to the movies on her own, a silly rom-com she'd hoped would clear her thoughts and raise her spirits, or at least distract her enough she could get some sleep tonight. It hadn't. She'd barely paid attention to the movie, and unusually for her, she'd even left half her bucket of popcorn uneaten.

Could she spend her life facing the grief of other animal lovers? Sometimes she'd help, sometimes she'd contribute to healing someone's beloved pet. But sometimes the only thing she'd be able to do would be helping them let go, helping a beloved animal die gently. After wanting this career most of her life, being focused on this one goal, on pursuing this path, she didn't know what she'd do with herself if she didn't stick with it.

What else could she be?

As she passed a narrow driveway next to a tall red brick building, a sharp sound caught her attention. From the parking lot behind the building, she could swear she heard…

A high-pitched squeal of pain had her dashing up the drive and barreling around the corner of the building, searching the gloom of the empty lot for the injured animal.

The last thing she expected to see was a huge man *kicking* a little baby Labrador pup.

After what she'd just watched a loving pet owner go through, the thought that someone would treat their own pet with such abuse made her see red. When the huge man kicked the puppy again, and the puppy let out another squealing whine, Cary charged in. She didn't even think about the fact that that huge guy might be dangerous to her. She didn't care.

No one should just kick a poor little puppy that way.

And she'd be damned if she stood by and let it happen.

"*E*nough," Cary roared, and swept the baby Labrador up in her arms. "What the hell do you think you're doing?"

"How I deal with this useless mutt is none of your concern, woman," the man said, his voice quiet, with a vague hiss to it.

Agh. She hated when men called her *woman*. It was just rude. "I'm making it my business, bub. I'm a vet." Only a partial lie. "And it's my sworn duty to protect helpless animals." Sort of. Technically.

He didn't need the exact details anyway.

The man growled at her, showing teeth which were very white and very pointed. And there was the faintest scent of sulfur coming from him, like he had rotten eggs in his pockets.

Weird.

"You do not know what you're meddling in, woman." He pulled himself up to his full height, which suddenly seemed even taller than before. His pale skin looked faintly green in the security light from the back of the building. "You will return my beast and be gone. Now."

His voice boomed out so deep from his wide, thick chest that his command reverberated between them like a base bell. She could feel the sound in her bones.

"No," she said, lifting her chin and dropping her head back so she could look him in the face. Geez, the guy must be seven foot tall. She snarled up at the puppy-kicker. "I will not allow the abuse of a helpless animal." She reached into her jacket pocket for her phone. "I'm calling 911. There are laws against animal abuse."

Some weird trick of the light made it look like the man's eyes were glowing red. That was really strange. She pushed aside the niggling voice in her head telling her that wasn't a trick of the light. Logically, it had to be.

Right?

"Drop the phone, woman, or I will make you suffer."

"Like you were making this poor puppy suffer? Yeah, no." She glanced down to dial 911. Even if the police weren't in a hurry to protect a puppy—which they should be—the guy had just threatened her. He was dangerous and the police needed to deal with him.

The huge man knocked the phone out of her hand, sending it careening to the ground. The crunching sound when it hit pavement made her wince.

"Bastard," she muttered. But when she looked up to give the man hell, the words died in her throat.

The puppy whined and tucked his head between her bicep and her chest. Cary swallowed hard.

The huge…thing before her no longer looked human.

Holy shit.

What was he…it…? What?

Horns like a ram's had sprouted from his head and curved up over his ears, his brown hair seemed to have lengthened and the tips of both horns and hair looked like they were glowing white. His eyes were most definitely red now, a bright, lava red. And his previously ordinary white skin was now covered in green and yellow scales.

What the ever-loving hell?

A scream clawed at her throat, as rough and brutal as scrapping sandpaper over delicate skin. Yet she couldn't make a sound. Nothing came out. The horror choked her. Suddenly, breathing seemed optional.

This had to be a trick of some kind. This was a mean sort of joke. The guy had just slipped into a Halloween mask when she was looking at her phone. Yeah, that was it. A mask. The bastard was trying to scare her because he was mean.

Mean enough to kick a puppy.

That thought ignited her anger again. How dare he try to scare her when he was the one in the wrong. She grabbed onto that anger and glared up at the guy she was positive was wearing a mask now.

"Tricks and a broken phone aren't going to scare me off," she said. "I'm not letting you hurt the dog. You don't want to get arrested for animal abuse, you need to leave. Now."

The man, who seemed even taller than he had a moment ago, like well over seven and a half feet tall—another trick she as sure— growled. Were his teeth even more pointy?

He raised a hand, pointing one very long finger at her. "You will die for your insolence, human."

She rolled her eye at the claw tips covering his fingers. "Those are very cliché," she said, pointing at his hands. "Really, with the ram horns and reptile scales, which I will say are a pretty scary mashup, the best you could do on your hands was fake claws?"

"I will melt your body. You will dissolve in pain and agony. And I will slurp up your juices."

"Ew. That's gross. Who says things like that? You really are a sick bastard. I'm no longer surprised you'd kick a puppy. But you're not gonna get away with that. And I won't be cowed by Halloween makeup and a gross threat."

A forked tongue slipped out between his hard-scaled lips as he hissed at her.

"Yeah, you started off original," she said, "but really, your costume has devolved into predictable. Maybe you should go back to the drawing board."

The man looked larger now and took a step toward her. Despite her brave words and her conviction that all this was a trick, she still stumbled backward a few steps. He stank of rotten eggs, so strong now the smell gaged her. And even before the stupid mask, the guy was huge. She wasn't exactly a tiny thing herself at 5'9", but he dwarfed her.

She really didn't want to get hit in the face by fists the size of this guy's.

But the puppy whined again, his little face burrowing deeper against her side, and her heart broke. Poor baby. She hugged him tighter and faced the looming threat. Fuck this guy with his horns and claws. He wasn't going to hurt this dog again.

The man lifted both hands, his too long fingers curved as he reached for her throat. Some kind of clear liquid dripped from his pointed talons, plopping to the ground with a faint sizzling sound. She didn't dare look down, but she was having a hard time convincing herself that was just bad stage glue melting out from under his claws.

"You're going to taste good," the man—man?—snarled.

"Gross," she said and took another involuntary step back, holding the puppy tighter in both arms now.

Unable to stop herself, she flicked a glance down at the ground. Sections of pavement the size of marbles had sunken in, the edges soft-looking, like the concrete had melted. She swallowed hard. That didn't look like a special effects trick.

She met the man-things blazing red eyes. His snarl turned into a terrifying grin and he laughed.

The sound made the hair on Cary's body stand up. She glanced behind the man toward the driveway, her only escape from the parking lot. But there was no way to get around him without getting close to his talons, and she was pretty sure whatever was dripping from them would hurt. She took a step to one side, hoping to give herself some space to run, but the man-thing blocked her way, his laughter loud in the quiet night.

The puppy howled in despair.

"Sorry," she whispered to the dog, giving him a gentle pat. "I tried."

3

———————————

he man-thing lunged at her with his dripping claws, too fast
for her to avoid. She folded herself over the dog, sheltering
him with her body even though she knew it was a useless gesture.

Wincing in anticipation of the pain, she squeezed her eyes shut. It occurred to her she probably should have tried running away sooner. But she'd never been good at running.

Her fight or flight instincts were really screwed up.

She'd gotten all the way through those thoughts before she realized the pain she'd been anticipating hadn't come. No dripping acid burning her skin, no deadly claws ripping her apart, no tearing or melting or… anything but a faint tingle dancing along her nerves, like static electricity during a lightning storm.

Really weird.

She squinted up at her attacker. He was snarling and hissing and throwing himself at her. But whenever he got within a few inches, he bounced backward. It would have been funny if she weren't so scared. She trembled with the fear, her knees so weak and wobbly she was afraid she'd collapse soon.

Yet, no matter what the man-thing did, he couldn't reach her. The liquid from his claws splattered around her, melting concrete like it was butter, but she remained safe inside an invisible bubble. One chunk of melted pavement did splatter up onto her jeans, burning a hole through the material over her calf and dropping against her skin. She stomped her foot a few panicked times to dislodge the pellet, kicking it away.

Given the stinging pain from that little chunk of half-melted stone, she could only imagine how much direct contact with the man-thing's acid would hurt. She had no idea what was holding him and his acid claws back, but she'd never been so grateful for anything in her life.

"Any idea what's happening here, little guy?" she asked the puppy.

He whined in response, but he did pull his head out from under her arm to look at the monster attacking them. The puppy sniffed the air, then leaned back into Cary. She was a little surprised to realize he wasn't shaking anymore. Her knees were still wobbling from all the adrenaline coursing through her blood. She gave the Lab a rub around his ears and he rewarded her with a lick across her hand. His tail thumped happily against her ribs.

After a few more attempted attacks, the man-thing snarled at her. "What are you? Some kind of witch?"

She stiffened her thighs to keep her legs from buckling and shrugged. "Haven't been before now." She was as baffled as the monster looked. "What are you, by the way? I'm thinking *not* a normal guy in a Halloween mask."

The thing hissed at her, his scaly lips pulled back in a threatening snarl. She winced and prepared for another round of attacks, keeping the puppy safely tucked against her body. The monster lifted his talon-tipped hands, the clear acid liquid dripped from his claws.

And then a look of utter shock moved through his expression. His red eyes widened impossibly large. His mouth rounded in an "o" of surprise.

He looked down at the ground, and Cary followed his gaze automatically. There was a very black hole under the monster, which made it appear like he was floating over empty space. He looked up at her, reached toward her and the puppy, opened his mouth as if to say something, and then fell into the black hole.

There was even a whoosh sound as the monster disappeared and the hole whirled closed.

For a very long moment, Cary just stared at the spot where the monster had been.

"Well that was weird," she said.

She had her eyes opened so wide they were starting to hurt. She blinked a few times, hoping the gesture might clear out her confusion.

"He was a demon," a rich, melodious voice said.

The sound pulled her attention up from the parking lot pavement. She spun around to face the newcomer. And blinked again.

The man standing at the far edge of the lot near the tree-lined fence was ridiculously handsome. Like the sort of handsome that only happened in movies starring Australia men playing gods.

Though this particular man was slimmer than Thor, he was still well-muscled and taller than her by a good four or five inches, making him at least 6'1" or 6'2". His pale blond hair hung like straight silk around his shoulders and his eyes were a deep green-blue that sort of reminded Cary of real emeralds—not those pale manmade things in all the jewelry stores now, but *real* deep green-with-a-hint-of-blue emeralds. He was wearing loose pants and a silk button down shirt that was open at the collar, which didn't look even remotely warm enough for the December night. His features were a little sharp but arranged perfectly.

He was just stunning.

She narrowed her eyes suspiciously. No one looked like that in real life.

Though, given she'd just seen someone dripping acid from claws after he'd grown horns and his skin had turned scaly, her definition of what people might look like in real life was evolving. Still. The ridiculously handsome man was far far too pretty. No one who looked like that could be trusted—especially when he'd just said something that only an hour ago she would have called crazy.

"A demon, huh?" she said. "As in those things that come from hell to torment souls?"

The stranger smiled, a super sexy smile Cary noted with a frown. It didn't reach his eyes.

"There are actually several demon realms," he said. "Hell is just one of them." He tilted his head to one side. "I should say hell is the name humans gave that one particular realm. The demons from there don't call it that."

"Okay," she said, easing backward a step. "Sure." She took another step and risked a glance behind her toward the driveway and beyond it the relative safety of the street. She'd waited too long to run when confronting the "demon." Running now seemed like a fine idea.

"Not curious enough to want answers?" the man asked, his perfectly shaped brows raised.

She stopped moving.

Damn him, she would like to know what had just happened. She did a quick calculation. Two minutes of explanation and if she was still feeling jumpy, she'd turn and run. She wasn't fast, but she could use the element of surprise. Out on the street, she'd just have to wave down a passing car and get someone to call the cops for her.

"What answers are you offering?" she asked. "Cause your last ones about demons and hell haven't left me with a lot of confidence in your information."

His grin widened, but looked a lot less calculating this time, like he was giving her a real smile and not an expression designed to get something from her. The humor reached his eyes this time.

Though she couldn't tell if he was laughing with her or at her. And since she wasn't laughing, she was inclined to think his amusement was at her expense.

"My name is Jaxer, by the way," he said.

He didn't offer his hand for a shake, which was reassuring. She didn't trust him enough to get within touching distance. "Cary."

"It's a pleasure to meet you, Cary," he said.

He sounded way too sincere. "Think I'll reserve judgment on that, Jaxer."

"Fair enough. Would you like a job?"

4

ary blinked a few times. The puppy in her arms let out a cute little woof but otherwise didn't comment.

"I have a job." She adjusted the now wiggling dog in her arms as he tried to lick her face. "And that wasn't an explanation for what just happened."

"Fine." He gave an elegant shrug. "The demon you confronted was attempting to escape his realm by going through this one and into another demon realm."

"How do you know that?"

"Magic," he said with a grin.

"Right. Magic." She scowled at him, knowing that wasn't the real answer. He looked too smug. "Continue with your explanation." She angled her head away from a puppy lick, using the gesture as an excuse to glance behind her, gaging her escape route.

"He stole the hellhound—"

The puppy interrupted Jaxer with a snarling growl that sounded a lot more vicious than a dog that little should make. Cary frowned down at the puppy.

"Sorry," Jaxer said. "Demon dog?"

The puppy grunted and snuggled into Cary's arms again, giving her hand a nudge and a lick until she started scratching behind his ears again.

"Demon dog, then," Jaxer said. "The demon stole the demon dog hoping it would get him into the new realm. Obviously, he didn't know enough about demon dogs for his own good."

"Huh?" Cary was too confused to run away now. It sounded like Jaxer was calling the harmless baby Labrador in her arms a hellhound and that made no more sense than a demon, or…

Well, actually, none of it made sense.

She looked at the puppy, who looked up at her, his little tongue lolling out one side of his mouth. She could swear he was smiling. And were his eyes… Were they brown or…red?

She stared into his sweet puppy face. "Demon dog, huh?"

The puppy woofed and waggled his tail.

"Well, you're awfully adorable for a demon dog," she said.

"Woof." And another tail thump of agreement.

That made her chuckle.

"I think he likes you," Jaxer said.

"I like him too," Cary cooed to the puppy. "But I think you need a name. Calling you puppy or demon dog seems too impersonal."

The tail thumped harder.

"Uhm…" Jaxer raised a finger to interrupt her.

She ignored him. "What name would you like? Fluffy?"

The puppy sneezed and shook his whole body.

She laughed. "Okay. How about George?"

"George?" Jaxer asked, sounding bemused.

The puppy sniffed and shook his head.

"Something less ordinary?" Cary asked. "Like Thermopolis? I could call you Thermy for short?"

Jaxer made a sound like he was choking on something. Cary continued to ignore him. Anyone trying to convince her this adorable Labrador was a demon didn't really deserve a say in naming him.

The puppy paused as if considering her last suggestion. Then shook his whole body again, like he was shaking off water.

"Okay, not Thermy," she said. "Do you have any suggestions?" she asked the puppy.

"He's a dog," Jaxer pointed out.

"According to you he's a demon dog," she said. "And he obviously has strong feelings about what we call him."

"Yes, about that…" Jaxer started.

Before he could finish, the puppy let out a deep bark. Not the woofs he'd been using up to that point, but a very distinct, "Baurk."

"Huh," Cary said. "That almost sounded like you said Buck."

The puppy woofed again, wiggling happily in her arms and scrambling up to try and lick her face.

She laughed. "Buck it is, then."

Jaxer groaned. "Well, he's yours now."

"What?" She finally glanced up at the too-handsome man with all the weird stories.

"You name a demon dog, you've claimed the demon dog as yours," Jaxer said with a resigned sigh. "I did try to warn you."

"Not very hard," Cary pointed out. "But that's quite all right," she cooed down at Buck. "Who wouldn't want to claim this cutey little boy. Aren't you a good boy?" She rubbed her cheek against his head and hugged him. She needed this puppy love after the day she'd had.

There was just one problem.

"Guess I'll need to go apartment hunting, though," she said. "My current place doesn't allow pets."

Buck's puppy growl made her grin.

"I can help you with that," Jaxer said. "If you'd like to actually talk to me and not just the dog." He sounded annoyed.

"Buck here at least makes sense. Nothing you've told me so far makes much of that."

"You just faced off against a man with horns and acid talons, and you don't believe what I'm telling you about him?"

"Fine, let's say you're not a crazy person and that was a demon. Why was he kicking Buck? How did his acid not burn me, except for that one rock? Where did the asshole demon go?"

Jaxer frowned. "You got hurt?" He glanced away and muttered. "Shouldn't have happened. Maybe…" Shaking his head, he looked back at her. "To answer your questions. He was kicking Buck trying to make him rip a hole in spacetime to open access into another demon realm. But immature hell— Sorry." He raised his hands palms out at Buck's growl. "Demon dogs can't open realm passages."

"Who opened the one that got the acid demon here?" she asked. This felt more like they were talking about a movie than a real-life event that had actually happened just ten minutes ago.

Jaxer shrugged. "An adult demon dog, maybe. Or he might have simply escaped the human who called him, and brought the demon dog with him to make realm transitions possible without human help."

"Simply? So demons can just come and go from this realm?" That sounded bad. Like really really not good.

Jaxer shook his head. "No, it's very hard to accomplish actually. And if he escaped the confinement of the human who called him, the human is likely dead."

"Ah. Okay. So. Uhm. None of this sounds…" What? Good? Realistic? Normal?

Possible?

She frowned at Buck. The dog in her arms was certainly real. She looked down at her jeans. There was a hole in the calf where there hadn't been one earlier. Jaxer seemed pretty solid even if he was unnaturally handsome. And there were parts of the pavement around her that had most definitely been melted.

She was starting to think this wasn't a dream.

But outside of adopting a puppy, she was pretty sure the rest of it sucked.

Before she could comment on that, Jaxer scowled suddenly, and a voice from just behind him said, "You've prepared her for her next assignment, Mentor?"

Jaxer rolled his eyes. "We haven't gotten that far. We've been busy naming a demon dog," he said, while still looking at Cary. Then he glanced over his shoulder toward the trees at the parking lot's edge. "And she's not ready for you yet."

"Who's not ready for what?" she asked, trying to look around him.

Jaxer sighed and stepped to the side.

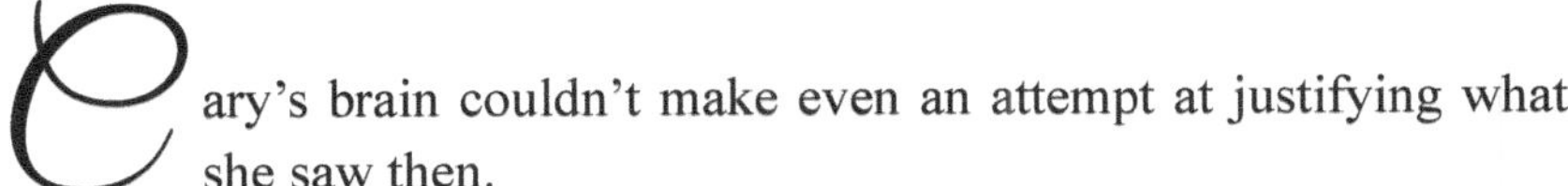

5

C ary's brain couldn't make even an attempt at justifying what she saw then.

The two…beings were awesome and so utterly strange she wasn't even sure if she could reconcile what she was seeing with actual words to describe them. They were beautiful in a very alien way.

One was mostly white and gold, with two golden horns poking out from a mass of white hair. Its—her maybe?—green eyes were glowing like they were lit from inside. The other one was mostly black and red, dark clothes, red skin, and a set of intertwined antlers that formed a halo on top of his head. This one also had glowing green eyes. Their eyes reminded her of the aurora borealis lights, a kind of green that was both natural and awe-inspiring and at the same time didn't look like it should be of this world.

She swallowed hard and hugged Buck a little tighter. This was turning into the weirdest night of her life. Maybe being a vet tech wasn't such a bad thing—at least it made sense.

"Protector," the white and gold being said to her, "you have accepted the powers. Jaxer will mentor you in your new role."

"Who what huh?" She shook her head hard, the way Buck had shaken his body when he didn't like a name suggestion. "Wait, wait…

What did you just call me? What powers are you talking about? I'm just an ordinary woman rethinking her career path and, you know, saving puppies from demons. Apparently. I didn't *accept* any powers."

"You didn't run," the red and black being said. He? He seemed to be projecting "he" anyway. He gave her what was probably supposed to be a reassuring look. "My name is Wisat. This is Liruk. Our people provide the magic for Protectors."

"Cool cool," she said. "Uhm? What's a Protector?"

"You," Liruk said. "Now."

"No. I'm just a vet tech."

Jaxer sighed loudly and raised his hands to silence everyone. "Liruk, she wasn't ready for you yet. Wisat, I'm still explaining how she accepted the powers." He looked at Cary. "Cary, the reason you weren't burned by the demon's acid was because you were willing to sacrifice yourself to save a puppy. That proved your worth to the Nagumwasuck and they, for lack of a better explanation, filled you with the powers of a Protector. We'll have more time to discuss the full details, but simply put, whenever you get between someone in danger and the something causing that danger, you will be able to protect the person—or animal—in need of help."

She straightened her shoulders. "That sounds… Good. Does it only work with magic stuff?" Cause if that were the case it was a little less impressive. There couldn't be that much magic danger going on in the real world.

Right?

She bit her lip and glanced down at the areas of pavement that had been melted by demon acid.

"It works against both magic and mundane attacks," Jaxer said.

"Like bullets?" she asked, without really believing that would be the case.

"Yes," Jaxer said, "like bullets."

She let out a sound that wasn't much more than an "Uhm." Even she wasn't sure what she'd meant.

"And you have accepted these powers," Liruk said. "You are a Protector now. It is your job and your duty."

"Whoa whoa whoa. I haven't accepted anything. I'm not accepting some job I didn't ask for and don't understand."

"You'll be paid," Jaxer said. "And we'll provide you with a home of your choosing—one that allows dogs."

She opened her mouth to say no, but paused. A house and a paycheck while she decided what to do with her life did seem conveniently helpful.

Jaxer smiled. She huffed out an annoyed breath. He didn't have to look so pleased with her reaction.

"What does this job involve?" she asked.

Liruk opened her mouth, but Jaxer spoke first. "Liruk and Wisat will send you on assignments to protect people. You protect them. I'll train and mentor you, so you won't be on your own. In exchange, good pay and a safe home for you and your new charge."

Cary narrowed her eyes. "I feel like there's a trick in there somewhere. A 'but' you're not telling me."

"Those are the basics," Jaxer said with a shrug.

"Why me?" she asked. "I'm pretty ordinary, and until about twenty minutes ago, I didn't even know demons and demon dogs and..." She glanced at the strange beings behind Jaxer. "Any of this existed. Why me?"

"You put yourself between danger and an innocent life," Jaxer said, this time sounding both sincere and impressed. "With no hope of success, you tried to save an innocent life. It was your instinct. You were born for this job."

She snorted. "I don't know about that." But the pay was very tempting. And the house. She'd like a house. She tilted her head. "I get to pick my new home, right?"

"You do. We can go house hunting first thing tomorrow morning." Jaxer grinned as if this was funny for some reason.

Cary glanced at Liruk and Wisat again. "No tricks? No catches? Just... I protect people from danger when you tell me to, and you pay me to do this?"

"Essentially," Jaxer said, giving the two beings a look over his shoulder.

She did need to do something while she re-thought her future and considered what she might want to do if she walked away from veterinary medicine. Protecting people and animals seemed like a nice way to make money in the meantime. And she could always quit if she didn't like the job.

"Tell me one thing," she said to Jaxer. "What the hell happened to the demon?"

"Oh, that." Jaxer waved a hand in a ridiculously urban gesture.

She rolled her eyes.

"He got pulled back into his original realm," Jaxer said. "Someone a lot stronger than he was didn't want him to escape." He shrugged as if that was obvious.

She opened her mouth to ask more. Then snapped it closed. Did she really want to know more?

Glancing down at Buck, she scratched his little head. "What do you think, boy? You think I should try this Protector thing for a bit? See how I do?"

Buck let out a deep woof and licked her cheek.

She chuckled. Then she met Jaxer's gaze. Those unreally stunning eyes in that unnaturally handsome face. "Mentor, huh? What does that involve?"

Jaxer smiled, his expression crinkling the corners of his eyes. "I teach you everything I know."

"Should I be afraid of everything you know?"

"I knew you were a smart woman."

"Right." She pulled in a deep breath. "I do need a new job…"

"It is done," Liruk said. "Mentor, begin her training. Protector, we will be back with your next assignment tomorrow."

She raised a hand to stop them but they vanished. One moment they were there, she blinked, and then they weren't there anymore.

"Tomorrow?" she asked the empty space where the beings had been. "I didn't actually agree to this yet, you know," she said to Jaxer.

"You'll be brilliant," Jaxer said. "Now, let's get you back to your current apartment, will we? You need your sleep. We have an early start to see about finding you a new home."

"My head hurts," she said, but fell into step beside her new mentor. "I'm going to wake up and discover this was all a dream."

"No," Jaxer said. "But don't worry. I believe in you." He dropped an arm over her shoulders in a friendly gesture.

She gave him a look. He grinned. Buck ignored Jaxer's hand on her shoulder and licked her face. She supposed Jaxer wasn't a threat if her demon dog wasn't growling at him. Dogs usually had good instincts about people.

"So, how do you know all this stuff?" she asked Jaxer. "How are you a mentor? How do you know those… What are they? My bosses now?"

"There's a lot to explain," he said with a reassuring pat on her shoulder. "I'll get to all of it. For now, it's enough to know that the Nagumwasuck are a species of North American Fae. They make Protectors. They're generally a good lot. Though Liruk can be a pain in the ass."

"Oh good. Fae, huh? Great. And what are you?" She winced. "You're not a demon too are you?"

"No. I'm also one of the Fae. I'm from two of the European lines."

"Of course you are. That explains everything. Especially your looks." She was only being a little sarcastic.

"My looks?" he asked.

"You're stunningly gorgeous. Real life people don't look like that."

"Think I'm gorgeous, huh?"

"Don't let it go to your head. I'm still pretty sure I don't like you."

He let out a booming laugh, the kind that came from the belly. The sound was so free and joyous, she had to force down her own bemused smile.

"Well, I like you my new protégé," Jaxer said. "I think we're going to have a lot of fun."

Cary glanced at Buck, then at the grinning faery next to her. Fun, huh?

Oh boy.

WHEN CARY MET PICKLES

A new job, a new house, a new demon dog... And so much to learn.

Cary Redmond has a lot of study ahead of her if she wants to survive her new job as a magical Protector. Study means books. And books mean spending time in a bookstore—something she will never object to. However, the place her mentor sends her isn't an ordinary bookstore. And the clientele are more than what they seem.

But with the help of The Bookstore's proprietor and the resident basset hound, Cary is sure she can navigate this new world without getting eaten by anything.

Maybe.

1

The bookstore wasn't on any map. Didn't have any obvious signs or displays to proclaim it open for business. And, Cary was absolutely certain, had never been on this street in all the years she'd lived in Portland, Oregon.

To be fair, she didn't come to this part of town very often, but she was pretty sure she'd have known about the little independent bookstore if it had always been here because she loved bookstores. The fact that this one looked, from the outside, like it belonged in this exact spot and had been here for a century was even more interesting.

The façade was simple painted wood, creamy white and clean despite the messy, rainy, muddy March weather. The door was oak and heavy looking, with a lovely brass handle. The name of the store—a little obviously The Bookstore—was etched in white into the clear glass of the store's large front window, but the text wavered, so it was hard to read unless she concentrated. Beyond the window, the store appeared empty. No displays of books. No piles of new releases.

The neighborhood was quiet, the streets lined with trees, and the car and pedestrian traffic pretty light for a mid-morning. The buildings surrounding The Bookstore were all small businesses, mostly for lawyers and accountants and realtors and the like. Businesses that didn't require a lot of foot traffic to keep them open and viable.

Unlike a bookstore.

Very interesting.

A lot about Cary's life was *interesting* these days. She'd somehow gotten tricked into becoming a magical Protector four months ago and her world had been strange ever since.

She still wasn't entirely sure what had happened. She'd been considering her career path, convinced she didn't have the constitution to continue working as a veterinary technician, she'd heard a dog in trouble, ran in to help, realized she was trying to save the puppy from a monster—which she learned later was a literal demon from a demon realm (not Hell apparently)—and next thing she knew, she and the puppy were fine and she was being offered a new job.

A job that paid, which was hard to argue with given she'd been considering a career change. Still, she never really did *agree* to do this work. Yet somehow, she now found herself running around getting between innocent people and danger, keeping those innocent people from getting hurt with magic she had no control over. It just worked when she needed it to.

Her bosses from a tribe of North American faeries gave her the magic. She channeled it. They sent her on missions. And she saved people. She was also mentored by this absurdly handsome, infinitely irritating European faery named Jaxer who'd helped her find a house right after tricking her into her new job.

It had been a weird few months. To say the least.

And now, here she was, standing outside a bookstore that should not have been there, looking for reference books for her new work library that was in her attic so when her parents came to visit, they didn't stumble across any incriminating evidence of her new career. Her mother would *not* understand.

Jaxer had given her this address, assured her this was the only place in town to find what she needed, and handed her a list of books to buy. She'd sourly told him he had the handwriting of a serial killer. She didn't actually know what a serial killer's handwriting looked like. It was just a line from a movie she liked and she knew he wouldn't get the reference. She spent so much time feeling off balance and out of her depth around Jaxer, it was good to throw him off his game occasionally.

Glancing around the quiet street, she pulled in a deep breath of damp air and pushed the brass door handle. There was a moment's resistance before the heavy door gave so easily she stumbled over the threshold, clattering into a bright, vibrant, and busy little bookstore.

Wait. Busy?

She frowned. She looked over her shoulder at the street outside. Then at the interior of the store. And all the people walking past the front window. And the piles of books displayed there.

Yup. Weird. Very weird.

The door closed behind her without much effort on her part. A small man in a long, old-fashioned duster bumped past her, apologizing with a raised hand and a distracted smile as he hurried to a shelf at one side of the store. She watched him for a moment, bemused. There was a tail peeking out of the bottom of his coat, a silky, hairy horse's tail.

She stood where she was for a long moment, just staring. Dark wooden bookcases covered all available wall space that she could see, and a few freestanding shelves filled out some of the middle of the store's floor space. Tables with piles of books took up additional floor space, giving the room a cluttered and crowded feel even though everything was well organized. It smelled like books and lemon wood polish, which was a really nice combination of smells. Maybe she could get her new attic office to smell this way with enough books. And some furniture polish which she didn't actually have at the moment.

The shelves were lined with volumes of different sizes, some leather bound, others more modern looking hardbacks. Not many paperbacks, she noticed. The tables were topped with faced out displays and sale signs. Over the bookshelves, the subjects were labeled with handwritten black cards, the text elaborate in silver ink and a type of calligraphy that made reading the labels a bit tough.

Did that one say "Sanguinary Theory"? How many books could

there be on a theory of blood? Apparently a whole shelf. Unless she was reading the label wrong. Although the tall, thin, suspiciously pale woman plucking books off the shelf kind of gave credence to the books being about bloodletting.

Cary suppressed a shiver.

She stood for a long moment, not moving, not entirely sure where to go. A cheerful face popped up in front of her, startling her back a step.

"Can I help you?" the woman asked.

She was a pretty dark-skinned woman with a gorgeous, fluffy afro and kind smile. She gave Cary the kind of blank helpful look a good sales clerk learns to master. If it weren't for the sparkling points of light like stars in the black depths of her eyes, she'd have looked like a perfectly ordinary human person. But Cary had the feeling there weren't many ordinary humans in this bookstore.

She might be the only one.

She held out the piece of paper Jaxer had given her with the list of books to look for and showed it to the star-eyed clerk. "I need to get these."

The woman looked at the list and nodded. "A nice selection." Her brows crinkled. "Diverse." She glanced up at Cary, a slight question in her expression.

Cary ignored the question and attempted to look innocent. She wasn't sure why she needed to look innocent. She wasn't guilty of anything. But Jaxer had warned her—especially in The Bookstore—to keep her job title and abilities to herself. Lot of things here with exceptional hearing and most of them dangerous. She couldn't afford to let many people know what she did because when she wasn't protecting someone, she was as easy to kill as any other human, and anyone who knew what a Protector was might also know that.

When she didn't satisfy the clerk's curiosity, the woman merely glanced back at the list and said, "Let's start in Demonology. We can work our way around from there." She led the way, weaving through the tables and shelves toward the back of the store.

Cary followed like a tourist, her head turning this way and that as she tried to take everything in at the same time. The store, once she started moving through it, was actually a lot bigger than it seemed on first glance. The back of the store extended deeper than Cary thought this building could accommodate based on the small parking lot next to it where she'd left her car. When a bell over the front door tinkled—a bell that hadn't been there when she'd walked in—she glanced back and realized the front of the store now seemed very far away. Wow. That was both weird and cool.

The person who'd just entered the shop stomped their feet loudly on the ground and appeared to brush something white off their shoulders. Snow? In March in Portland? It had definitely not been cold enough for snow when she'd walked in.

"This is your first time here, right?" the nice clerk asked.

Cary faced forward again. "Yeah. I hadn't realized the store was here."

"Well, 'here' is relative with The Bookstore." The clerk nodded back at the door without looking at it. "We're not exactly locked into a space-time location in the usual way."

"Uh huh," Cary said, because she wasn't sure what else to say and was too overwhelmed by the idea of the store not being locked into a specific location to come up with a more intelligent response.

"Here's everything we have on Demonology," the clerk said. "You'll find those first two books here. When you're ready to look for the next things on your list, let me know. I'll be floating around."

Without meaning to, Cary glanced down to check if the clerk actually was floating.

The woman gave a soft, knowing chuckle. "My name is Renee, by the way."

"Nice to meet you. I'm Cary Redmond."

"Welcome to The Bookstore, Cary Redmond," Renee said. "Just look up when you need me again."

Renee headed back out onto the main floor, walking—not floating—toward the person who'd just entered the store.

It occurred to Cary the floating comment might have been a test of some sort, one that she'd failed, but since Renee hadn't seemed either offended or upset, Cary let it go.

This wasn't the first test she'd failed since getting this job anyway.

2

Cary studied the Demonology shelf with a mixture of fascination and horror. So many books. So. Many. The implication that the subject was this huge was…scary. Very very scary. She looked at the list in her hand, picked out the first title: *A Beginner's Guide to Basic Demonology*. Yeah, she needed that.

After a search, she found a copy sandwiched between *The Definitive Catalogue of Demon Phylogeny* and *Demon Phylogeny Updated to Accommodate Liam's Findings and Death*. She hovered a hand over that second book. The too-long-but-very-descriptive title was hard to resist. But she'd better get the basics down first, before she tackled the academic advancements that came about because of "Liam's Findings and Death."

Though she was really curious to know who Liam was.

With her Beginner's Guide in hand, she started the hunt for the next book on her list. A gentle nudge around her calf made her glance down. A big-eyed, long-eared, thick-bodied basset hound looked up at her. The dog had been standing to get her attention but when Cary looked at it, the dog plonked down into a sit, its thick tail wagging a little.

"Well hello there," Cary said. She squatted down to give the basset

31

a scratch behind the ears. The dog leaned into her hand. "You the store dog or a shapeshifter I should be more leery of?" she asked quietly.

"That's Pickles," Renee said.

Cary glanced up. She was pretty sure the store clerk hadn't been there a moment ago. "Pickles? What kind of name is that for a basset hound?"

Renee shrugged and grinned at the dog. "Technically, she's a foo lion."

"A palace guardian, huh?" Cary turned back to look at the basset whose tongue was hanging out of the side of her mouth in what looked suspiciously like a smile. "Are you guarding The Bookstore now?" she asked Pickles directly.

Renee answered. "Actually, she sort of does. Mostly, though, she's here because she lost her mate. Foo lions typically travel in pairs, you know."

Cary hadn't actually known that, but it was good information to have. "I'm sorry you lost your mate," she said quietly to Pickles.

Pickles let out a very sad, and surprisingly recognizable, sigh.

Renee leaned around Cary and scratched Pickle's head. "She's a good friend of The Bookstore, aren't you Pickles?"

Pickles's answering woof was deep and resonant.

"Why a basset hound?" Cary asked.

"That's the form she wanted to take," Renee said. She chuckled. "And I'm not going to argue with a palace guardian."

"Fair enough," Cary said, with feeling.

Pickles looked on as if all this conversation was irrelevant to her existence. Which, Cary thought, it really was.

"Do you need help yet, or still working your way through the demonology texts?" Renee asked, straightening and flashing one of her beautifully perfect helpful clerk smiles.

"I'm still coming to grips with demonology," Cary said. "Thanks."

"Call when you're ready for help," Renee said.

Cary gave Pickles one last ear scratch then went back to her book hunt. Pickles flopped on the floor at her feet, heavy jowls resting on the floor. The company was surprisingly comforting given the sense of overwhelm creeping through Cary as she examined the rows upon rows of books on subjects that covered the complete spectrum of supernatural and preternatural phenomenon. All stuff she was expected to learn.

This felt substantially more impossible than learning everything she'd had to learn to get her biology degree.

Pickles accompanied her around the store, waiting patiently with her as she went through her list, then lifting up and trotting beside her as she moved on to a new shelf and a new subject. Cary had only made it through about a quarter of the list—a heavy stack of twenty hardbacks and three old leather-bound volumes—when she decided she needed a break for the day. Under normal circumstances, collecting twenty-three books in a bookstore would have felt liked she'd won the lottery. But the more she explored, the more she knew she had to learn, the more overwhelmed she got.

What the hell had she gotten into with this new job?

Renee rang up her purchases at a central counter with a very modern-looking computer register system topping it.

The hair on the back of Cary's neck prickled the entire time she stood at the register, but she tried to ignore it. She hadn't felt nervous about her surroundings earlier. And the sensation wasn't the one she got when someone needed her brand of magical protection. So she figured it wasn't something she needed to worry about. It felt like someone was watching her. Probably just someone as curious about her as she was about most everyone else in the store.

Still. There was an edge to the feeling. A very vague sense of… She wasn't sure. Maybe a threat? But since her, admittedly new, magic wasn't giving her a warning, she wasn't sure she was reading the situation right.

Despite telling herself to ignore it, she kept glancing over her shoulder, trying to spot the person—creature?—staring at her.

Renee watched her as she entered the price of the various books into her computer. "You're safe here, you know?" she said quietly. "This store is neutral ground. That's strictly enforced or we'd go out of business. Right, Pickles?"

From below the counter, where Renee wouldn't have been able to see her, Pickles stood from her flopped sprawl and woofed. The woof sounded like a very clear yes.

Cary grinned at the dog that wasn't a dog.

Out of curiosity, Cary asked, "How exactly is the neutral ground rule enforced? Everyone's on their best behavior or they get banned?"

"That works for some," Renee said as she started slipping some of the books into a large paper bag with twine handles. "The book worms and information junkies won't risk getting banned. Most of the wizards and witches observe the honor system without trouble because information and knowledge are required for them to do what they do."

Renee took two of the leather-bound books and started wrapping them in brown paper, rather than putting them into the bag with the others. At Cary's slight frown, Renee smiled.

"These don't play well with other books once they're out of the store," the clerk said. "You'll need to keep them on a separate shelf." She held up the paper wrapping and a shimmer of words appeared. A warning about storage rules and strict instructions on how to not die while using the books.

"Ah," Cary said. Why the hell had Jaxer told her to get those? "I'm not sure I'm set up for something like that. I'm really new to all this."

"Don't worry," Renee said. "The paper will keep them sealed and safe. Just don't unwrap them until you feel comfortable." She winked and went back to getting all the books ready.

Cary bit her lip, not sure if this was a good idea or not, but what the hell. She could always give the books to Jaxer to keep safe. He'd deserve that after sending her here to get them without warning her they might be dangerous.

She pulled out her wallet to pay, but the sense of being watched made her pause and glance around again. No one seemed to be looking at her. Cary frowned. Maye it was one of the books? Now that she knew some of them were obviously more than just paper and ink, she supposed it was possible she'd just attracted the ire of one of the more malevolent works.

Even the idea of that weirded her out. She faced the register again.

Renee returned to the earlier conversation. "We have other ways to keep everyone here in line," she said. She reached under the counter and pulled out a brown leather tote with The Bookstore stitched in white on the front. She held it up. "Bring this back the next time you come in and you get a ten percent discount." She put the paper wrapped books inside. "There are spells around the store that help the more volatile shifters remain focused. Some scent and pheromone dampening things to keep the creatures that normally fight with each other from getting triggered. And of course, if anyone does get out of line, there are death spells—depending on what they do of course." Renee was quick to say.

As if Cary might be worried about the deaths spells getting some poor innocent monster.

Actually, she was a little worried about that and was grateful for Renee's clarification.

"The threat of death, or in the case of some of the beings, banishment to realms they don't want to be in, is enough to keep everyone cooperating. I think most of them like that this place is neutral and they're safe here. It's like a little bit of peace in an otherwise dangerous life for some people."

Her tone softened at that last in a way that made Cary think she might just be talking about herself. "I'm glad it's safe here," Cary said, meeting Renee's gaze. "For everyone."

The clerk smiled and took Cary's money.

Just six months ago, Cary would have had a minor heart attack handing over that much cash for a stack of books. Her new job, for all its weirdness, sure did pay better than her last. Although, she suspected that was hazard-pay since the likelihood of her dying in this job was significantly greater than her likelihood of dying when she was just a vet tech.

As she took her packages and receipt from Renee, she said, "I'll need to come back since I'm not finished with my list." She glanced around. "Will the store still be in the same place or...?" She let her question trail off mostly because she wasn't entirely sure what she was asking.

Renee came around the desk to walk her to the door. Pickles kept at her side as well. Cary realized after a few steps that with Renee on one side of her and Pickles on the other she no longer felt that weird sense of tension she'd been sensing at the register. Interesting.

"Whenever you want to come back and visit, you're welcome," Renee said. "We'll be right here." She winked.

Pickles woofed.

"Well thank you," Cary said to the basset. "And thank you," she said to Renee. "For all your help. This has been a very illuminating shopping trip."

"Glad you got some of what you were looking for. We'll see you soon." She opened the door, and the chilly Portland breeze blew in, scented by the Willamette River a few blocks away.

Cary shook her head. "How does it know to open in Portland?" she asked in a quite tone. "I mean, could I...get out somewhere else on accident?"

"Nope. The door links your DNA signature to your location. You can only ever exit back to the place you entered." She shrugged. "Keeps others from using the store as a shortcut to invading another realm. Remember to bring back the tote for a discount."

3

***

Cary returned to The Bookstore three days later, her list in hand —with a few more books added because the standoff with the gnome the day before had left her confused. A gnome bad guy. Who knew?

Obviously, she still had way too much to learn.

To her delight, Pickles met her at the door.

"Hey, girl." Cary squatted down to doggie level to give the basset a scratch behind her ears.

She should also pick up a book on foo lions, she decided. And maybe one on demon dogs, since she'd recently become the fur mommy to a demon puppy, who took the form of a golden Labrador and for the most part acted like an ordinary adorable, but mischievous, puppy. She kept forgetting Buck was a demon dog. Except when she accidentally used the word hellhound, which he hated. But still, she should learn more about his breed.

"What do you think, Pickles?" Cary asked the basset hound. "Should I get some good doggie books while I'm here?"

"Woof," Pickles said.

"You're absolutely right," Cary said, straightening. "But first, I'd better find that gnome book Jaxer suggested." She glanced at Pickles, who was following her through the store. "Did you know gnomes could be bad guys and might try to throw sharp wooden stakes they produce out of thin air at you?"

"Woof," Pickles said, her tail wagging.

"Of course you knew," Cary said. "You live in a bookstore."

Pickles flopped onto the floor next to Cary's feet when Cary stopped at a shelf. The basset's jowls spread out onto the ground as she laid her head down, and her thick body seemed to flatten. She looked inordinately comfortable on the wooden floor. Cary grinned at her before turning her attention to the shelves.

"Welcome back," Renee greeted a few minutes later, stopping beside Cary to replace a book high on the shelf. "You didn't get through all those books you just bought already, did you?"

Cary snorted out a laugh. "It's gonna take me years to read everything I need to read. No, I just thought I'd better get some more to add to the stack."

"Well I'm always happy to have a return customer," Renee said. "Let me know if you need any help."

"Thanks."

Renee strolled away, her presence leaving a sense of calm in her wake. That was nice. Especially since there was a creature with yellow eyes studying the shelf next to Cary, and she was pretty sure that hairy person she could just see from the corner of her eye to the left was a Yeti.

This was the wildest bookstore she'd ever been in.

She could get used to it.

With Pickles accompanying her through the store, Cary picked up another ten books. She eyed the stack and considered how much she didn't know. She really wasn't sure about this new job of hers. Most of the time, she felt totally inadequate to it. She was just an ordinary woman, and this job kept throwing her into a pretty extraordinary world that she knew next to nothing about.

To shut down the feeling of overwhelm, she decided she'd better call it a day and headed toward the register, just as the store's front door swung open. A huge man stepped through, maybe seven-foot tall, with heavy brows, a thick jaw line, and a nose that looked like it had seen better days. His dark hair was silky smooth and hung to his shoulders, practically glowing in the store's overhead lighting. His hair was a weird contrast to the harder, rougher look of his face. The combination of that plus his height really made him stand out. Cary paused in mid-stride to gape at him.

He narrowed light colored eyes and scanned the store. His lip lifted in a snarl when he looked at Cary. When he spotted Renee, he grinned.

Cary's spine tingled a warning. One she was starting to know well after four months of working as a Protector.

She set her stack of books down on a nearby table and started moving closer to Renee, who was standing at the "Mystical Locations" shelf, helping another customer.

Renee frowned at the newcomer's grin and turned to face him. Her customer, a tall thin man with pointed ears like an elf, wearing a Hawaiian shirt and board shorts, looked between Renee and the huge man, then started edging the opposite direction.

In fact, everyone in the store seemed to have gone on full alert and were subtly ducking behind shelves and tucking into corners. From her peripheral vision, Cary even caught one woman fading into invisibility.

Whoa. That was cool. She'd have to ask about that after she stopped the looming fight.

While everyone else edged away, Cary snuck closer, trying to keep her movements slow so she didn't call attention to herself. To her surprise—or maybe not given the basset's real incarnation—Pickles edged along with her, keeping right next to Cary's ankle, her movements surprisingly silent in the now very quiet store.

Renee broke the silence first. "Nar'el. We've discussed this. I gave you a choice last time you were here. You chose to stay away."

"I lied," he said, his voice a loud, booming echo.

That voice fit his face, Cary thought. Not his hair, but definitely his face.

"So I see," Renee said and sighed.

"You're no longer fit for this job, Rye-Nee," he said.

Cary frowned at his pronunciation of Renee's name.

"Since it's mine," Renee said, "that's not your call." She stepped forward, toward Nar'el, and swept her hand from a position over her head all the way to the floor.

A column of orange light dropped down and encompassed Nar'el. He snarled and pushed against it, but the wall of shimmering light held, keeping him captive.

"Now," Renee said, "I warned you that I would ban you permanently, and you didn't heed me. That's unacceptable."

"You're letting *humans* in now," the man snarled and glanced at Cary.

Cary froze. What, her? Wait. She was somehow the cause of this?

"We've always let humans in," Renee said, sounding amused. "Wizards. Witches. Psychics. All sorts of humans come and go."

"But she's ordinary. Mundane. Nothing that belongs in our haven. *Our* haven." Nar'el pushed against the barrier again. A few sparks of light flared around his hand.

"This has nothing to do with her," Renee said. "She's your excuse. You've always wanted my store and the knowledge here for yourself. You think the others will support you now." She gestured to all the current customers hiding in corners and behind shelves, staying out of the way. "They won't. This is my place. I keep it neutral. And I say who's allowed. Not you."

"You can't hold on to the store forever, Rye-Nee. The last owner fell. So will you."

"He retired and left me the place. I didn't engage in a hostile takeover."

"He's dead, isn't he? A rather permanent retirement."

"The only kind of retirement our kind gets," Renee said, sounding both sad and resigned. "And since we've aired all this in front of all my customers, despite my efforts to keep it private so as not to embarrass you, I will finish with the fact that you don't have the power to hold this store together or maintain control of all the diverse magics. That's why Pat chose me."

"Paa-tra was an idiot," the man snarled.

"You think everyone who's not you is an idiot, Neil."

"Don't use that name," he hissed.

"Stop using my old name," she countered. "Makes you sound ancient and out of touch."

Cary pressed her lips together to hide her grin because she didn't want to draw their attention.

Nar'el—Neil Cary thought with amusement—threw himself shoulder first against the column of light. He didn't have much room to move so there wasn't a lot of momentum in the act, but a wash of sparkles lit brightly around him as he slammed against the barrier. The column held.

Cary frowned slightly at the containment light. It reminded her a little of those transporter beams from that science fiction show. Only it didn't vanish. She'd better ask what that was when all this was done. Her bosses and Jaxer would expect her to know about this kind of spell eventually.

If it was a spell. For all Cary knew, it was just some super high-tech security system made out of laser beams or something. Which would also be cool.

She risked a glance down at Pickles as Renee tisked at Neil's efforts to break the beam.

Pickles was still on her feet, watching the exchange, but she didn't seem particularly tense. It could be hard to tell with a basset hound. They looked pretty mellow and relaxed most of the time. But Pickles seemed unconcerned with Neil's efforts to escape the containment beam. If the foo lion wasn't worried, Cary figured she could relax too. Renee had this handled.

Still. Those damned tingles continued to crawl along her spine, warning that her Protector magic was needed. A leftover of the adrenaline rush from when the standoff started, or a real warning? She was still too new to the feeling to be sure.

Neil slammed against the column of light one more time.

Renee crossed her arms over her chest and shook her head. "Are you done yet?"

Neil started to laugh. The sound made someone hiding behind the table closest to Cary gasped. A collective indrawn breath seemed to sweep through the store. Pickles came to full alert, her body stiffening, her tail pointing up and vibrating slightly, her nose straightening toward Neil.

Cary looked around nervously. Uh, everyone else seemed to know something she didn't. At a guess, she'd say Neil didn't usually laugh.

Renee narrowed her eyes at the man. "Time to go," she said and lifted her arm.

Before she could complete the gesture, Neil raised a hand and pressed it against the column of light.

The column burst apart in a shattering of brightness sharp enough to cut.

Screams erupted around the store, melding with the sound of exploding glass and the stink of burnt ozone.

Cary covered her eyes to shield them from the flare. When it faded, she blinked at the scene. Renee was on the ground at the base of the shelf behind her, blood—green blood!—dripping from her nose and a series of cuts across her arms. As if she'd actually been cut by the light from the column's destruction.

Cary rushed to her, getting between her and Neil. "Are you okay?" she asked.

"Get out of the way," Renee screamed, reaching out to shove Cary aside.

Cary dropped to her knees and held her spot, despite Renee's substantial push. "No, it's okay. Take a few breaths. You're hurt." She had a feeling, under different circumstances, Renee could have tossed her aside easily.

There was a collective gasp throughout the store again, and Cary saw some lights flaring around her from the corners of her eyes, but she kept her focus on Renee. "Can you move?" she asked. "How badly are you hurt?"

She should have gotten between Neil and Renee earlier. Damn it. She'd waited too long, and Renee got hurt because of her hesitance. She'd be kicking herself for that later.

Renee blinked at her. Another flare of blue-white light encompassed them but remained at a safe distance so they weren't injured by it, whatever *it* was.

Cary glanced over her shoulder to see a very angry looking Neil with his hand raised, palm facing them. She got a brief view of a circle of metal centered in his palm before light flared and barreled toward them. It slammed against her Protector magic and splintered around them harmlessly.

Neil roared.

Cary ignored him to concentrate on Renee. "Are you going into shock?" Cary asked. She held up her fingers. "How many am I hold up?"

Renee frowned slightly and shook her head. Then her eyes widened. The stars in her dark irises flickered and sparkled like the flashes of a meteor shower.

"Ah," she said, her shoulders relaxing. "I hadn't realized before but that makes perfect sense."

"What?" Cary asked.

"You're not a witch."

"Oh, yeah. I'm not a witch."

Renee glanced around. "I'm not sure if anyone here will know what you are, but best keep it between us I think."

"Yeah, I was told that was…safer."

"Indeed," Renee said. She glanced around Cary's shoulder to where Neil was raging and still trying to kill them. "He's stolen something he shouldn't have," Renee said. "That medallion in his palm. It's too dangerous for someone like him." She shook her head. "He's going to kill himself." Her smooth brow creased. "Oh hells, he might blow the whole place apart right along with him."

"Can you contain that explosion?" Cary asked. "Cause, I'm not sure I can. I'm pretty new to this. I think I can keep everyone here safe if I can get between him and the rest, but everyone is scattered and…"

"And the store's nature complicates things," Renee finished for her. "Yes, it does." She huffed. "Unfortunately, I can't risk hitting him with either my powers or the stuff the store can do without risking blowing us all up. Damn it."

Panic started to creep through Cary's chest. She looked around at all the scattered bookstore patrons and started motioning to them. "Get over here. Get behind me. Hurry."

Several people looked at each other frowning. A few hurried without question to stand next to Renee. Cary stepped a few feet in front of them, forcing the continued blasts of light energy from Neil's hand backward. He shouted something in a language she didn't know and tried to push forward.

Cary narrowed her eyes against the glare, and focused on motioning more people behind her. She glanced back long enough to see Renee on her feet again, frantically gathering up her people into a loose group. A few hold outs refused to move, which made Cary's panic spike. She couldn't get to them without opening the people already under her protection to danger.

Frantic for a way to get them closer, she screamed over Neil's continued noise, "Get over here!"

She blinked, and suddenly the holdouts were behind her. Renee frowned at them and said something under her breath, pointing a finger at them like an irritated teacher.

Cary wasn't sure if Renee had moved them or they'd moved themselves but she was extremely grateful to now have everyone in the shop safely behind her. She faced Neil again. He was looking at the disk in the center of his palm, his heavy brows lowered over his pale eyes.

Renee came up to Cary's shoulder. "You keep him from blowing us up," she said. "I'll try to hold the store together."

"That would be great," Cary said. Neil was starting to glow the same blue-white as the energy he'd been fire at them earlier. "I owe you a drink if we survive this," she said to Renee.

"You're now permanently on the 'friends and family discount' list after this," Renee said.

"Cool."

Neil's huge body started to tremble and the skin along his arms split open, scattering green blood.

Gross. Cary glanced away.

And realized in horror that Pickles was still outside her protection.

5

"Pickles," Cary called. "Get over here, damn it."

"The store's not going to hold," Renee shouted. "He's releasing too much rogue energy."

"Pickles," Cary yelled.

The basset hound glanced her. Neil screamed. The skin on his face ruptured, splattering more green blood. His bones showed through his remaining skin, like the image from an X-ray scan superimposed over his real face.

Cary urged Pickles to hurry, waving both hands at the dog in a frantic motion.

Pickles glanced back at Neil as more of his skin split apart. The disk in his still extended hand was glowing white hot, the heat washing over Cary even at several yards away. She raised her arm to block the heat and light from her eyes. The stench of cooking meat made her gag.

She looked at Pickles again, wanting to cry when the damned dog refused to move. "Damn it, Pickles," she shouted. "Get. Over. Here."

"The store's gonna go," Renee said, her voice strained and harsh.

Cary braced herself for the chaos to come, hoping her Protector magic would at least keep the people behind her safe, even if the store around them crumbled. She gave Pickles one last pleading look, then felt the ground under her shake and couldn't focus the basset hound anymore because she had to concentrate on staying upright. She watched Neil's disintegrating body through narrowed eyes, wincing as she prepared to take the bulk of the blast.

Suddenly a huge figure rose up beside Neil, with a head as big as a car. It had a vaguely stylized lion look to it, with a thick tawny mane around a face that seemed to blend cat and dog features with a short muzzle and dark tipped nose. The eyes were huge saucers of darkness. The pale, fur-covered body of the creature was thick and long, heavily muscled. Its four legs ended in paws the size of a mini-fridge with wickedly sharp talons fully extended.

The creature loomed above Neil. Neil with what little sense he had left looked up at the creature. The creature opened its mouth wide, revealing a row of huge, sharp teeth.

And then it ate Neil.

Cary blinked. The creature dropped that open mouth right over the top of the exploding bad guy, closed its mouth and gulped once, swallowing Neil whole.

The ground stopped shaking and silence descended over the store, broken only by the sounds of a few remaining books dropping off shelves and hitting the wooden floor with a thud.

Cary stared at the creature that had just eaten Neil. It let out a belch and a puff of green-blue smoke emerged from its mouth. It plonked its butt onto the ground, looking for all the world like a docile, friendly monster.

Then it shrank back to the shape of a basset hound.

"Pickles?" Cary said. Cary looked around to make sure everyone else had seen what she'd just seen. Then she looked back at the basset hound. "Did you just eat the bad guy?"

"Woof."

"Well," Cary said, blowing out a breath. She glanced at Renee. "She stopped him from exploding on us and tearing the store apart, right?"

"She did," Renee agreed.

"In that case." Cary looked at Pickles again and smiled crookedly. "Thanks for your help."

"Woof."

Cary rubbed her hands over her arms as a rush of tingles like static electricity shivered over her skin. That happened sometimes after a protection involving magic. It was a really strange sensation that left her insides dancing for a few minutes before her body settled back down.

Renee frowned a little at Cary's gesture. "You okay?"

"Yeah, sure. Just a little post-shielding-against-magic reaction. I'm fine." She shrugged. "I didn't just swallow a bad guy whole." She gave Pickles a look. "Will she be okay after that? I mean…that can't be good for her digestion."

"Woof," Pickles said and belched again.

The smell of the belch traveled and Cary waved a hand in front of her nose to dispel the stink.

"The ways of the foo lion's digestion are a mystery," Renee said in a philosophical tone.

Cary snorted.

Pickles laid down on the floor with her face resting between her front paws, her jowls spread out, looking as philosophical as Renee had sounded.

THE NEXT FEW MINUTES INVOLVED A LOT OF ASSURANCES THAT everyone was okay, and some milling about without any idea what to do next. Eventually, Renee got everyone settled and, somewhat to Cary's surprise, they all started helping with the cleanup, reshelving all the toppled books.

"You have a nice place here," Cary said.

Renee smiled and shook her head. "Most of the time, it is."

Cary glanced between the remaining customers and Renee. "So, since I'm pretty new to all this, would you be able to, maybe, explain what just happened?"

"Beyond Pickles eating Neil?"

"Yeah, that part was pretty self-explanatory." If not a little gross.

"Neil's been trying to take this store since before it was mine. The previous owner knew he wouldn't be a good fit for the place. The store is… Well, it's sort of its own thing."

"Like, a living thing?" Cary asked, fascinated.

"In its way. It has to like the proprietor, that's for sure. And there's always an initial stage of, shall we say, feeling each other out. The store tests. The proprietor either passes or fails."

"What happens if you fail?"

"You die," Renee said with a shrug. "Neil was never going to pass. Pat, the previous owner, knew that and that's why he chose me to take over."

"What was that disk thing Neil was using to fight your magic?" Or technology. Cary hadn't exactly established which it was yet.

"Something he stole from the ancient ones and should never have tried to control. Idiot." Renee huffed out a disgusted breath, settling her hands on her hips. "If he couldn't control the store, he sure as hell didn't stand a chance against an elder coin."

"Elder coin?"

Renee waved that away. "It's complicated. Suffice it to say, it was beyond Neil's pay grade."

"Fair enough." Cary raised her brows. "Wait. Pickles swallowed that coin when she ate Neil. Is that going to hurt her?"

"Believe it or not, no. She's just contained it. Which conveniently puts it out of reach of any other would be people intent on a hostile takeover of the store." Renee glanced down at Pickles. "She'll probably throw it back up at some stage."

"Woof."

"Or maybe not." Renee shrugged as if it didn't matter either way.

Cary gave Pickles a doubtful look. Pickles returned the look with one of stoic confidence. Given how little she knew about foo lions, Cary would have to trust Pickles and Renee knew what they were talking about.

She hesitated over her next question, stalling by putting up another book. She wasn't sure whether she should ask this or not. But what the hell. In for a pound.

"Can I ask something that might be a little personal?"

Renee tilted her head in polite patience.

"What *exactly* are you? And Neil." Given they both had green blood, Cary was assuming they were the same species.

Renee glanced around the store. The others were still shelving books but a few were obviously listening to the conversation, their attention too focused on the shelves while their bodies leaned toward Cary and Renee.

In a quiet voice, Renee said, "It's better I don't discuss that." Even quieter, she said, "Just like it's better no one knows *exactly* what you are."

Cary looked at the milling crowd—if that one guy wasn't a Yeti, he really should be—and nodded. "Yeah, that's smart." She faced Renee. "You know, though, right?"

Renee smiled. "Thanks again for your help."

"Any time," Cary said. "Apparently, it's what I do now."

6

Once the store was back in order, Renee rang up Cary's books —which had fallen under the table where she'd left them but somehow managed to stay mostly together—and true to her word gave Cary the friends-and-family discount. A handy twenty percent off.

After confirming Renee liked wine, Cary promised to bring a bottle on her next visit to make good on that drink she owed Renee.

Pickles followed Cary around during all this, sticking to her side as Cary helped clean up and then as she paid for her books. The basset ambled along next to her and Renee as they went to the front door.

"Thanks for your help," Cary said to the dog that wasn't a dog.

Pickles licked her lips.

"That's gross," Cary said with a grin that leaned toward a wince.

"Woof."

She shook Renee's hand and headed out, blinking in the sunlight. It had been cloudy when she went into the store. The early spring sun was a nice change, if a little bright after the softer indoor light.

Cary turned to wave to Renee and realized Pickles had walked out of the store with her and had moved a foot down the sidewalk in the direction of the parking lot.

"Uhm." Cary glanced between Renee and Pickles. "Is she just escorting me back to my car?"

Pickles sat on the sidewalk, patiently waiting.

"She hasn't left the store since she moved in," Renee said, her brows raised. "I don't know what she's doing."

"Woof," Pickles said and she stood, turning back toward the small, narrow lot beside the bookstore. She paused next to Cary's Corolla's back door and woofed again.

"I think she's going home with you," Renee said.

"Wait, what? I thought she was yours."

"Pickles is her own," Renee said. "I have no say in what she does. Never have."

"But…" Cary hurried to her car. "Pickles, sweetie, I'd love to have you come stay with me, but I literally just adopted a demon dog a few months ago. And, well, can you two live together? I mean, will a foo lion and a demon dog get along? He's still just a puppy so, you know, he might be a little…exuberant." She shrugged. "I don't know. Will that work?"

"Woof," Pickles said and batted at the car's back door.

Renee patted Cary on the shoulder. "She's going with you, one way or the other. I'm sure she and your hellhound will get along fine."

"Oh, don't call Buck a hellhound," Cary warned both Renee and Pickles. "He hates that."

"Woof," Pickles said and wagged her tail. Her tongue hung out to one side of her mouth, making it look like she was smiling. Then she batted at the car door again.

"Looks like you've just adopted a second dog," Renee said in an amused tone.

Cary glanced between her and the basset hound. She gave in to the inevitable with a resigned sigh. "Looks like I have. Good thing I have a backyard now."

Renee chuckled. "Just be careful what you feed her." She winked. "Oh, and if she does throw up that elder coin, you can bring it back here. I'll take care of it. Just be careful how you handle it."

Cary lifted a finger and opened her mouth to ask more questions, but Renee had already turned back toward the store.

"See you soon, Cary Redmond. And good luck."

Cary looked down at Pickles. Pickles grinned up at her.

With a shrug, Cary opened the car's back door. The basset hopped in, defying her short legs to scramble up onto the back seat. She settled in like she owned the car and waited patiently for Cary to close the door and climb into the front.

"Ready to go home?" Cary said into the rearview mirror.

"Woof," Pickles said, and laid her head down between her front paws, her jowls spreading out. She thumped her thick tail twice against the seat.

Cary chuckled and started the car. She was now officially the fur mommy to a demon dog and a foo lion. Her world had gotten very, very strange in the last few months.

But she supposed there were worse ways to live.

Pickles belched quietly. Cary cracked the window and tried not to think about Pickles's last meal. She'd better find something healthier for her new charge to eat.

What did you feed a foo lion besides bad guys?

"What do I feed you besides bad guys?" she asked the dog.

She glanced at Pickles in the rearview mirror again. Pickles thumped her tail and appeared to wink. Cary raised her brows.

Oh boy.

WHEN CARY MET MARIANNE

All women need more pockets in their clothes…

Except Cary Redmond has found in her new job as a magical Protector standard pockets do not hold up to the abuse. After losing her keys—again—she seeks the help of a friend from her pre-Protector life. Marianne is an animal lover, a devoted fan of 80s music, agrees wholeheartedly that pineapple does not belong on pizza, and best of all, is a seamstress.

Their friendship was meant to be.

But there is more to Marianne than meets the eye. And in this new world of magic and mayhem, Cary is learning everybody really does want to rule the world.

1

Technically, Cary first met Marianne Johnson at the veterinary practice, when Cary still thought she wanted to be a veterinary technician. Marianne volunteered there at the weekends and they'd hit it off immediately. Talking about their mutual love of animals led to talking about their mutual love of 80s music and movies, which had led into conversations about food, which then led to a discussion on the best pizza toppings, and when Marianne agreed that pineapple on pizza was a sin, Cary knew she'd found a soul mate.

But when Cary left her job as a vet tech after being tricked into becoming a magical Protector (at least she got paid for the Protector stuff), she'd lost track of Marianne.

Unfortunately, Cary's new job had proven to be seriously damaging to her wardrobe. She'd lost count of the clothes she'd had to replace over the last six months. After losing her keys *again* out of a torn pocket, she'd decided she needed to do something about the things she wore to work.

And when Marianne wasn't volunteering with animals, she was a seamstress with her own boutique in the Pearl.

Cary pushed open the glass door to the shop, the little bell overhead dinging as she walked into the cool, brightly lit interior. Polished, spotlessly clean hardwood floors gleamed in the overhead light, the pale color complimenting the cream walls. There was a register and desk to one side, a door covered by a purple curtain at the other, and a series of floor length mirrors near the curtain. A long table with neatly stacked bolts of material took up most of the open floor space in the front of the shop, along with a row of comfortable looking chairs near the register. The whole place smelled of cloth, hot steam from an iron, and cinnamon. It was late in the day, almost closing time, and growing darker by the minute outside, but inside felt all light and airy and cozy.

Cary loved the shop immediately.

She carried the jacket she needed repaired folded over her arm—another sad casualty of her job. This time the entire back had been shredded down the middle by a lunging werewolf. Cary had gotten between the wolf and his intended victim, a stunned-looking woman who turned out to be a lower level wizard, just before the werewolf reached her throat.

The wizard had been minding her own business, just coming out of a local fast food restaurant, when the wolf attacked. It had taken some time to get the story out of the enraged wolf, but it turned out he was having trouble shifting between his forms and kept getting stuck in partial shifts which were painful—and impossible to hide—and he blamed the wizard for cursing him.

As far as Cary knew, wizards didn't work in curses. That was the domain of witches. But she still had a lot to learn about all this magic stuff. An entire attic of books as a matter of fact.

At any rate, the poor wizard didn't even know the man, nonetheless try to curse him. She claimed not to know anything about werewolves either. Given her shock, and the fact that the Nags—Cary's bosses—had sent her to protect the woman, Cary tended to believe her. Later, she had quickly double checked in one of her many attic books, though. Just in case. And it turned out, she'd remembered right. Wizards didn't do curses.

Her faery mentor, Jaxer, had taken charge of the werewolf, promising to get him help, and Cary had escorted the wizard safely home. Which was when she'd discovered that not only was the back of her jacket shredded, the bottom of one pocket had been torn out, and with that, Cary's house and car keys had been lost to the streets of Portland.

Again.

After the first time that had happened, she'd left spares at her house. But still, this was getting ridiculous. She'd lost her keys five times in only six months. She'd lost her wallet twice and had learned to keep only the important stuff in her pants pockets. Also to always wear pants with pockets—she'd made that mistake once too. But the whole thing had gotten out of hand. She had to do something.

She wasn't sure *what* exactly. Maybe zippers on her pockets? Reinforced material?

"Cary Redmond! What are you doing here? Where have you been? They said at the veterinarian's office you quit."

Cary turned with a grin to greet Marianne as she came into the main shop through the purple curtain. "Hey, your hair is magenta now!"

Marianne kept her tightly curled hair in a short cut she called a tiny weeny afro. The close-cut style suited her—she had the bone structure for it—and, as Marianne had said, was very low maintenance for a busy woman. But she did like to play with color.

"I like it," Cary said, hugging her. "How have you been?"

"I'm great. What happened to you?" She was dressed in a pair of gorgeous flowing tan linen pants and a fitted, short-sleeved white shirt that complemented her dark complexion and looked perfectly tailored to her curves.

Which, Cary thought, it probably was given her business. "I was having a career crisis moment, so I took another job while I considered what I wanted to do with my life."

"I get it," Marianne said, leaning lightly against the large table strewn with bolts of material. "It's hard when any pet has to be put to sleep. I can't imagine helping with that day in and day out. That's why I just volunteer. I like petting all the cute kitties and puppies."

Cary chuckled.

"So what brings you to my little kingdom?"

"I need help," Cary said with a sigh. She showed Marianne her jacket.

Marianne let out a low whistle.

"This is happening a lot in my new job. And I keep losing my keys out of my pockets. I can't even carry a purse. So I need a way to keep everything in. Zippers? Even a few extra snap buttons might help."

"What on earth are you doing now?" Marianne said, examining the long slashes in the gray denim. "This looks like a wild animal got to it."

"Yeah." Cary sighed. "Something like that. Can you help?"

"Of course. I can do amazing things with needle and thread." She winked.

"Thank you," Cary said. "I'm really getting tired of losing my keys."

"Mm hm," Marianne muttered, fingering the ragged edges of material and frowning deeply. "I can fix anything, but this will take some work. You want me to repair and update this jacket or just make you a new one."

"You can do that?"

Marianne tucked her chin and gave Cary a look.

Cary held her hands up in surrender. "Thanks," she said. "A new jacket would be great. More than I was hoping for."

"I don't work cheap, but I can give you a friends-and-family discount." Marianne went to the register counter and started typing up the invoice on her computer.

"Don't worry about the money. You have a business to run, and I can afford full price. My new job pays well."

Marianne grinned at her. "I'm glad to hear it. Better than being a vet tech?"

Cary blinked. "Actually, yes."

But she considered the extra money hazard pay. Jumping in between good guys and bad guys definitely qualified as hazardous.

Marianne printed out a sheet of paper, picked it and the now useless denim jacket up and motioned toward the back room. "Shall we go take some measurements and pick out material?" She wagged her eyebrows like picking material was on par with eating ice cream.

Maybe for Marianne it was.

They were almost to the back room when the little bell over the door dinged again. Cary turned with Marianne to see the new customer.

2

—————

A little man with a fox-like face stood just inside the shop. He was maybe four foot two, wiry thin, bandy-legged, wearing baggy pants and an oversized sweater. His skin had a faintly gray cast to it, his dark gray hair was thinning and uncombed. His eyes were dark, almost black. When he smiled, his teeth were surprisingly white against his almost black gums, and a little pointier than Cary might have expected.

Marianne sighed, put her free hand on her hip, and said, "How many times do I have to tell your impy-ass to leave me alone? I'm not helping you."

"You will, you will," the man said, his voice high and squeaky. "You and your sisters are needed. You will. He sent me for you."

"And you can tell him no. Again. I'm not spinning gold for that bastard."

"Spinning gold?" Cary asked, looking between the little man and Marianne. "You can do that?"

Marianne waved a hand in the air. "Think of it as a metaphor."

Okay. Cary narrowed her eyes at the little man.

"He said you should come or else," the man said, with a slight laugh that sounded reflexive more than amused.

"Or else what?" Marianne said. "I am not his servant to call whenever he likes."

"Who's *he*?" Cary asked.

"This asshole king who thinks I'm here to do his bidding," Marianne said.

"A king?" Cary said.

"My king will have his way," the little man said.

This was all very weird, Cary thought. Although, after six months of her new job, her definition of weird had altered radically. She just hadn't been anticipating weird at Marianne's shop.

Marianne pointed a finger at the door. "Leave. I have a customer. I don't have time for this nonsense."

The little man giggled again, then pulled something out from the hem of his sweater. Cary had just enough time to recognize it as a crystal ball, a very small one, maybe the size of a baseball, and as clear as a water bubble. The man's smile widened into something truly horrifying.

And then he threw the ball at Marianne.

Instinctively, Cary stepped in front of her friend. She wasn't even sure what she was blocking, but sure enough her powers worked because the ball stopped a few inches in front of her face and just hung in the air, vibrating.

So. Obviously a threat then.

Cary blinked when it swung to one side, then another, as if it were trying to find a way around her.

And not an ordinary glass ball.

"How are you doing that?" Marianne asked.

"Long story," Cary said. "Part of the new job. What the hell is that thing?"

The ball swung back a few feet then came flying at them again. Cary put a hand on Marianne's arm to keep her from moving. She flinched when the ball got as close as a few inches from her nose before stopping abruptly.

The little man started dancing around and stomping his feet. "No no no. It's supposed to work. Why isn't it working? You have to come with me. He insists. He wants his gold."

"This is really weird," Cary commented.

"Look who's talking," Marianne said. "Since when do you have magical powers?"

"What makes you think this is magical powers?"

"The fact that that crystal ball is magic, and you're standing there keeping it at bay."

"Oh. Yeah. That. How do you know the ball is magic?"

Marianne let out a long breath. "I've seen him use them before. Didn't think the bastard would actually use one on me."

"That's going to require a longer explanation," Cary commented as the ball flew to the opposite side of the shop and then barreled back toward them, moving so fast it left a musical note in its wake and rainbows dancing across its surface. It might have been pretty if it hadn't been flying at them at deadly speeds.

"Uhm." Cary half glanced over her shoulder at Marianne. "If that thing actually gets close to you, what happens?"

"I'll get sucked inside."

"Okay. Well. That's not good."

"No, it is not."

"Then what?"

"The imp will take me back to the goblin king, and the king will try to force me to weave his damned gold."

"Also sounds bad—mostly because you don't sound like you want to do that."

"I don't. Amongst other things, the bastard uses the gold to trick parents into handing over their children. It's gross."

"Ew. Yeah, it is. Do people actually give up their children for gold? That seems... Well, a bit fairytale-ish."

"A lot of the time, they trick the parents or guardians into it, but yeah, some do it willingly for the gold. The king hands over fake stuff, which turns to iron the minute the goblins have the kids. But the king really hates humans. He uses real gold at first, to bring out their greed. Then does the switch."

"That's all awful."

"Which is why me and my sisters are not going to help him." She sighed. "Guess the cats out of the bag."

"About goblin kings and the fact that you can weave gold?" Cary asked.

"The fact that you aren't calling me crazy and screaming how this is impossible gives you away, you know."

"Oh." Cary frowned. "Gives *what* away exactly?"

The imp started stomping closer then, waving his hands around. "This works, do you hear me. This works. You have to come back. How can you stop the trick? It's a king's trick."

Cary shrugged. "Just talented I guess. But you're not allowed to kidnap my friend so you should just, you know, go away. And tell this king of yours that Marianne is not going to help him."

"No no no! He will rule the world. This must work." The imp stomped his foot on the floor so hard it made the windows tremble.

Cary glanced at them, worried his tantrum might break the glass. The crystal ball chose that moment to fly toward them again, from the side this time. Marianne gasped, but Cary still had a hand on her free arm so she wouldn't move away. Cary winced as the ball trembled in the air a few inches from her temple.

Then in a shower of light and glitter—glitter?—the crystal ball exploded. Tiny silver and gold flakes sparkled across the stores pristine floors.

3

"**W**ell shit," Marianne said. "That's going to be a pain to clean up."

Several of the flakes landed on Cary's arm. The fact that they'd gotten onto her and didn't hurt was a pretty good sign—at least she hoped—that the glitter was harmless. She blew the sparkly dust off.

"The spell broke?" she asked Marianne, just to be sure.

"Spilled magic all over my floor." Marianne sighed again. "But yeah, it's no longer dangerous."

"Oh good." Cary looked at the imp.

He was staring at her wide-eyed, his mouth hanging open. "How did you break the king's crystal?"

"No idea," she said with a shrug. "But that's going to be the last of this nonsense. Right? Tell your king to leave Marianne alone. She's not his seamstress."

"Weaver," Marianne corrected.

"Weaver?"

"That's the technical term for my gift."

"Oh. Cool." Cary met the imp's dark, narrowed gaze. She narrowed hers in return. "I will just keep blocking your king from getting at my friend. Tell him that. Tell him he is done here."

"I can't I can't I can't," the imp said, starting to stomp around again. "No no no. This must work. This must bring her back. The king needs more gold. He will rule the world. We will rule the world!"

"No," Marianne said at the same time as Cary said, "I'm not allowing that."

"Your king has got enough gold," Marianne said. "Greedy bastard. And he's got more than enough goblins. He doesn't need to keep stealing more. He's certainly not going to rule the world."

"No, he is not," Cary added.

"I won't help him," Marianne finished.

"See," Cary said. "And I won't let the king force her into helping him. The answer is no."

The little man roared, though it sounded like the pouting cry of a child—still vicious and scary but without a lot of moral high ground behind it.

"He'll deal with you," the imp said, snarling at Cary. "You've made a powerful enemy."

She shrugged. "Not the first time." She glanced back at Marianne. "I suspect I'm gonna make more in this new job, too."

Marianne patted her shoulder. "It's okay. You do good work. That's all that counts." She looked at the angry imp. "I think we're done here."

From a pocket in her pants, Marianne pulled a long iridescent clothe. Like a magicians trick, a lot more material came out of her pocket than should have reasonably been there. The gossamer clothe had a pearlescent sheen, dancing with blue and pink light. It looked insubstantial but also like it could envelope everything—a colorful kind of fog.

"What's that?" the imp asked before Cary could.

"A present for your king," Marianne said.

She twisted the material between her hands, rolling it around in a swirl that mesmerized. With a flick of her wrists, the thin clothe floated away from her in a gentle fall that landed on the staring imp. He blinked as the material settled over him, staring at them through its thing folds. His eyes suddenly widened, he opened his mouth, but before he could speak, the material fluttered, and the imp vanished from beneath.

The material floated gently to the floor.

"Wow," Cary said. "That was some trick. Where did he go?"

"Back to the goblin realm," she said. "Transportation clothe is good stuff."

"Yeah, it is." Cary titled her head. "So, weaver, huh? I've never heard of that particular skill. What, exactly, does it mean?"

Marianne didn't pretend to misunderstand the question. "I've got the good magic," she said, wagging her eyebrows. "I can do a lot of interesting things with needle and thread. And yeah, yeah I can spin flax into gold." She waved that away. "But that's boring."

"Sure. Of course it is." Cary grinned. "I take it you prefer things like magic pockets?"

"I do. Every woman should have pockets in her clothes, and magic pockets are all the better."

"I agree! How much extra for the magic pockets? Cause, I could really really use those."

Marianne smiled. "I got you. And the first two magic pockets are free. You know, because you saved me from getting kidnapped and all."

"Deal."

"Now," Marianne said, turning her toward the back room, "what *exactly* do they call your magic? Cause I'm thinking it's not witchcraft."

"Nope. It's hard to explain. But you can think of me as…a walking Kevlar vest. I get between good guys and bad guys and keep the good guys safe."

She technically wasn't supposed to tell people what she did, or how it worked. For her own safety. Her powers *only* worked when she was protecting someone. When she wasn't, she was as vulnerable as any human. The less people who knew what she was and how it worked, the better. But given Marianne had a secret power of her own, Cary figured she could give her the basics.

"That's your new job?" Marianne said. "I'm impressed. I want to hear more about it. But after we get your measurements." She faced Cary, her eyes widening. "I didn't tell you. Gina got her club open finally! You have to come see it."

"She got the last of the funding? That's amazing." The last time Cary had spoken with Marianne, her girlfriend was still working on getting enough start-up money together to open the nightclub the way she wanted.

"They do an 80s night," Marianne said. "Every Sunday. That would be tomorrow night."

"Oh, I am so there."

"Then over a few drinks, you can explain a little more about this new job of yours."

"If you explain more about being a weaver."

"That's a fair trade. And I have a feeling you're going to need more from my loom than just a new jacket."

Cary glanced down at Marianne's superbly tailored linen pants and the pocket that had produced the transportation clothe. There wasn't even a hint that that pocket might contain more than it looked like it could. No bulges. No break in the smooth lines of the pants.

Yeah. She definitely needed magic pockets. Lots and lots of magic pockets.

WHEN CARY MET ANGIE

For Cary Redmond, sometimes the mayhem really is all about the magic...

After only a few months as a Protector, Cary's got the basics of the job down. Get between the good guy and the bad guy. Good guy survives. Everyone's happy. Except the bad guy, of course, but they don't really count.

Introduce magic into that equation, however, and Cary knows she's out of her league. A magic problem needs a magic solution. And while the super powerful witch who comes to her aid isn't exactly what Cary expects, she'll take all the help she can get. She might even survive the night, with a little help from her newest friend.

1

———————————

The shapeshifter was fast. So fast, she could barely see him when he moved.

Cary's Protector powers gave her all the skills she needed to protect good guys from bad guys, but there was only so much magic could do with an otherwise ordinary human body. Seeing this guy clearly when he ran was more than her eyes could manage.

Though she could now see the *blur* that was him in a way she couldn't have just a few months ago.

She wasn't even sure what kind of shifter he was because he was still in his human form, but damn the man could move. In her—admittedly short—time as a Protector, she'd never actually seen anything else that could move that way.

The dim street lighting didn't help. The area was blessedly quiet as this street was lined with the kinds of businesses that closed at reasonable hours. So she wasn't worried about innocent bystanders. That, however, was the only thing she wasn't worried about.

She'd barely gotten between the guy and the teenager he attacked in time to keep the poor girl from getting her throat ripped out. Cary's heart still thumped hard in her chest at the close call. Too close. She didn't dare take her eyes off the shifter as he raced around her and her charge, looking for an opening, but Cary was sure she'd just ruined another jacket. The shifter's fingers had definitely connected with more than just air as he grabbed for the girl.

Fortunately, because of the magic her new bosses had so recently given her, the shifter had been tossed up against a nearby building before he could do more damage than just rip the collar off her coat.

"Any idea why this guy is going for your throat?" Cary asked the trembling kid behind her.

The girl couldn't have been more than seventeen. She had a pretty, round face, straight black hair, and dark eyes which were currently too wide against her too pale complexion. Her fear made Cary's chest tight. She wanted to pat her arm and assure her everything would be fine. But Cary wasn't entirely confident of that fact yet.

"I was walking home from a study session," the girl said. "I don't know what he wants. He works for my uncle, but we've never even spoke. He just... How does he move like that?"

The girl said something in Chinese that Cary didn't understand because she generally sucked at languages and wasn't having any luck at all with the language-learning part of her studies for her new job. Then the girl screamed and gripped the back of Cary's coat as the shifter launched at them again.

His eyes glowed with a sort of watery blue light, which Cary found strange for a shifter—their eyes usually glowed yellow or gold. But she was so new to all this, she couldn't be certain if that was unusual or not.

He hit Cary's protective barrier, bounced backward into the building behind him again, and dropped to the ground with a thud that made Cary wince. He shook his head and lifted his lip in a snarl. She raised her hands, palms out, hoping to calm the manic attack.

"Look," she said, "you're not getting to the girl. All that throwing yourself at us is just going to wear you out. You might as well stop and go home. Leave the girl alone. For good. Although, her uncle is probably going to fire you for this."

The girl's grip on her coat tightened.

The man snarled, but something in his eyes made Cary frown. It looked like the watery glow dimmed and there was something else there. She looked closer, trying to pinpoint the emotion but before she could name it, the glow increased and the shifter charged them again. This time her magic sent him flying into one of the trees lining the sidewalk.

Cary sighed. "This might take a while," she said to the girl. "He's going to have to wear himself out before he'll be reasonable enough to discuss this. In the meantime, why don't we talk a little? My name's Cary, by the way. Cary Redmond."

"Suzy Pang." The girl's voice trembled and was barely audible above the shifter's snarling.

What the hell kind of shifter was he? Cary wondered. Aloud, she said, "You're in high school, right Suzy. What grade?"

"Twelfth. B-but I'm taking two classes at Portland State, getting some extra credits. I want to be able to s-skip freshman year of college like my...my big sister did."

"That would be handy," Cary said. "Save a lot on tuition." She'd been a good student but not nearly good enough to skip grades or get ahead on her college classes while still in high school. She choose not to think about the student loan money she might have saved. "You must be very smart. What were you studying tonight?"

The girl squeaked as the shifter threw himself at her from the side. Cary's magic encompassed her and the girl fully, though, so he couldn't just sneak up behind them or get a new angle on his attacks and get around the barrier.

"Was it for the college class?" Cary asked, working to distract Suzy.

She wasn't sure how long it would take this guy to get tired and go away, but she didn't want the poor girl to pass out from fear. In the few short months Cary had been doing this job, she'd found keeping her charges distracted with boring small talk really helped them calm down. Keeping them as calm as possible meant they let her protect them.

Everyone came out of the situation a lot better when her charges *let* her protect them.

"No," Suzy said. "This was for my physics class." Though her voice was quiet, the trembling had lessened enough that she wasn't stuttering her words anymore.

Cary took that as a win. "I loved physics, but I sucked at it," she said. "Vectors. I could never get the hang of vectors."

Suzy laughed a little. "I love physics. Especially astrophysics. I want to be a physicist. But…"

"But?"

The shifter charged again, slamming so hard against Cary's shield, it looked like he'd hit a window, leaving his face smashed against midair, his hands pressed against the invisible wall.

She finally got a better look at him. Dark hair, a handsome face, light tan skin, the typically fit shifter physique. He was younger than she'd at first thought, though. Maybe not much older than Suzy. Cary frowned at that.

"My parents want me to be a doctor," Suzy said. "Or go into pharmaceuticals. They think those fields have more job potential."

"My parents are the same," Cary said. "Parents always want you to have a secure job. They worry when they think you're doing something less stable."

"Yeah, that's exactly it. Plus, my older sister is a microbiologist working for a big research company. She's very successful."

"Ah, having to live up to a more successful sibling." Cary nodded. "I get that too. My sister is getting married in a few months. She's my *younger* sister. I'm hearing a lot of 'why don't you settle down' now from my mother."

Suzy giggled. "I don't get that yet. But only because Jenny isn't married yet either."

"You're lucky," Cary said. She watched the shifter closely as he finally started to slow down, moving at human speeds now. He stalked a back and forth pattern in front of them but was no longer throwing himself uselessly at her shield.

Cary risked trying to talk to him again. "As you can see, getting through me is impossible." She hoped. She had to rely on what her faery mentor, Jaxer, told her about these powers she'd been given. "Why don't you calm down and we can talk, huh? Let's start with… Why are you attacking Suzy?"

"Don't know," he said through clenched teeth, his jaw tight. His voice was deep, rough, like he'd overused it. "Can't stop."

2

"**W**hoa," Cary said, raising her hands. "Wait...what? You're not doing this on purpose?"

He shook his head but it looked like it took effort to make the movement.

Well, shit. What did she do now?

"Jaxer," she said aloud, "I could really use your help. What the hell is going on here?"

The North American Fae who made Protectors and who were Cary's new bosses—she called them the Nags because they were—had sent her to protect Suzy Pang. They hadn't given her the girl's name, just said get to this corner in the Sellwood-Moreland neighborhood immediately and protect the "girl," but that was all the information they'd seen fit to give her.

Cary had written that lack of detail off to urgency. The situation *had* been urgent. And she'd had to get all the way across the city. She'd barely arrived in time to throw herself between the shifter and Suzy.

But given this man—boy really—didn't want to attack Suzy, something a lot spookier was going on.

"You have any control of your animal right now?" Cary asked him.

He nodded in one hard jerk. "Can stop the shift," he ground out.

"Can't stop…" He threw himself at her barrier again, the glow in his eyes intensifying.

This was so weird. And she had *no* idea what to do. She needed to help the man, but she couldn't do that without putting Suzy at risk, which was unacceptable. And she was here to protect Suzy anyway. But still.

"What did you mean by his animal?" Suzy whispered.

"Oh, right. He's a shapeshifter. Not sure which kind yet. But definitely a shifter."

"I… Those are supposed to be stories. Fiction."

"Yeah, I know. Lot of stuff I thought was fiction turns out to not be. Hey, maybe you can work the physics of it all out one day?"

"Uh…"

Suzy didn't sound too sure of that career path. Cary couldn't really blame her. Probably not a lot of job security in it.

The glow in the young man's eyes dimmed, and he looked at them with an expression so tortured Cary's heart ached.

"Is some*one* making you attack Suzy?" Cary asked him.

"Why would someone want to hurt me?" Suzy said in a quiet voice. "I'm no one."

The man raced a circle around Cary and Suzy, then suddenly, in one of those too-fast-to-see moves, he was up in one of the sidewalk trees. Cary blinked, looked up in time to see him there, then he dropped onto them, like a big cat in the jungle.

She even squeaked this time, and put a hand on Suzy's arm to keep her from bolting. The shifter hung in the air above them, snarling and thrashing, his teeth snapping toward them. It looked really really odd. Then he slid to the sidewalk a few feet away, landing on his feet gracefully. He was sweating hard, his t-shirt soaked through. And the strain stretched his skin tight over his bones.

Boy, she could use Jaxer's help right now. He said he'd be here soon. He was *supposed* to be helping her.

The shifter threw himself at her again, but slower and with a lot less backlash. He was finally getting tired, which was hopefully a good thing.

Cary blinked as a strange thought occurred to her. If she could walk closer to him, maybe get him into a corner, bracketed in by her powers, maybe she could somehow…protect him from whatever was driving him to attack Suzy against his will?

Would her powers even work that way?

She held onto Suzy's arm and said over her shoulder, "We're going to walk toward him. Don't panic and run. I can keep you safe, but only if you stay with me. Okay?"

She felt Suzy shiver. "Why are you going to get closer to him?"

"He's in trouble here, too. I'm hoping if we can maybe hem him in, we can disrupt the… I don't know. Whatever it is that's making him do this."

"Will that work?"

That was the million dollar question.

Keeping Suzy close to her back, she edged toward the young man, holding his gaze as she did. The blue glow faded just a little and he jerked his chin down once, like he was agreeing to this plan. At least, that's what Cary thought she saw in his expression. He backed away, keeping a few yards of space between them, but he didn't try to run or circle her. Even when the blue glow intensified and he started snarling at her, he didn't try to escape her approach.

She wasn't sure if that was good or bad. But she almost had him backed up against the brick and glass office building at his back. The windows in the building were all dark this time of night, the neighborhood relatively quiet. A good thing because Cary hadn't learned how to protect her charge and still keep innocent bystanders safe yet. She wasn't even entirely sure how many people she could protect at once.

Huh. She'd better ask Jaxer about that.

When the young man's back touched the building, he snarled, his hands coming up to reach her. But he couldn't get at her so he just clawed the air in front of her face. He seemed pretty tired, like he wasn't putting much effort into the attempt anymore.

Which was good?

Unless… "Are you fighting the compulsion to attack?" she asked him, taking one step closer to see what would happen.

He nodded and snarled some more. She watched him closely, taking another step forward. This time he hissed, a vicious sound that rose from a deep place, and razor sharp claws flicked out from his fingertips before retracting.

Okay.

Cat shifter of some kind then. As far as she remembered, there were leopards, a few cougars, supposedly some jaguars, and exactly two tiger shifters in the greater Portland area. No lions that she was aware of, but that was just based on the last demographics tables she'd read. That didn't mean there weren't any lions in town. Just that they hadn't filled in their supernatural census forms. Or whatever shifters did to get into the books she was studying when she wasn't protecting people.

Now that she thought about it, how did one go about getting a census of supernatural creatures? Most of this world was kept secret from ordinary humans. Was there like an underground government organization that researched these things? She'd better asked Jaxer about that, too.

The shifter hissed again and then let out a yowl of pain, pulling her attention back to him.

"Whoa, am I hurting you?" she asked. "What's wrong?"

She hadn't moved any closer. And once he'd backed up against the building, he hadn't really tried to escape. She wasn't even close enough to keep him in place in any real physical sense. Given his speed and strength, he could have gotten away. Instead, he was pressing his hands against the bricks of the building behind him, yowling and hissing, his head thrashing back and forth.

Cary started to panic. This didn't look good and she didn't know what to do. Did she back away and give him some space? But if she did that, would he just run off? Or worse attack Suzy again?

"Hey," Cary said, raising her hand to try and get his attention. "You in there? What's happening? Do you need me closer or to back up?"

He screamed then, so loud Cary winced and Suzy covered her ears.

Shit.

Cary made a move toward him, but he was obviously still a threat to Suzy because as Cary got closer he was forced farther back against the building. To her amazement, some of the bricks cracked, leaving a disconcerting line of damage running up the side of the building.

She took a quick step backward. She really didn't want to bring an entire office building down on accident. She didn't know if she could do that or not, but she wasn't about to risk it.

"Well. Now what?" she asked the air.

"I might be able to help," said a voice from a little farther up the street.

3

*C*ary turned toward the newcomer, carefully keeping Suzy behind her.

A tall, thin woman stepped out from behind a tree into the street lights. She had curly, light brown hair pulled back into a ponytail, a few beaded braids hanging around her pale face, and she wore a swishy, multi-colored skirt under a patchwork coat. She looked like the stereotypical pagan hippy, right down to her Birkenstock sandals and tinkling ankle jewelry.

Cary shook her head at the sandals. It wasn't unusual in the Pacific Northwest to see people in sandals in the winter. But really, it was too cold tonight for Birkenstocks without at least wearing a pair of socks. The woman's toes were going to freeze off.

"Hi," Cary said. "You might want to stand back. Got a bit of a situation here."

The woman smiled, a bright expression that crinkled the skin beside her green eyes. She was a really really pretty woman, the kind of striking beauty that belonged on a magazine cover.

"Probably should introduce myself," she said. "I'm Angela Jordan. Call me Angie. Jaxer sent me."

"Oh. Cool. I think. Why?"

Angie walked closer, her attention on the still thrashing shifter. "Him," she said. "I take it he's fighting the spell?"

"Spell?" Cary asked.

"Spell?" Suzy echoed in a whisper.

"A compulsion spell," Angie said. "Nasty one by the looks of it." She mumbled something under her breath. Then stepped a little closer to the young man who hissed viciously and swiped out in her direction.

Cary moved to stand between him and Angie, while still keeping Suzy close. "Uhm, you probably don't want to get too close. He might be fighting whatever is making him do this, but he's still pretty dangerous."

Angie nodded. "Thanks. Actually, if you could stand there keeping me safe for a minute, I might be able to break the compulsion."

"Oh? Well, yeah, then. That'd be great." Cary glanced at the woman. "You're a witch?"

"Yup."

"Handy," Cary said.

Angie fell silent and Cary darted her gaze between the hippy witch and the struggling shifter. She glanced back once or twice to make sure Suzy was still holding it together. To Cary's amusement, the teenager was studying Angie with the kind of fascinated look Cary had seen in other biologists in college when studying a particularly interesting new species. The bug people got that look a lot. Intent and focused, watching carefully to see exactly what the newly discovered bug might do.

Cary wasn't sure Angie would like the comparison to a bug, but Suzy was definitely fascinated by whatever Angie was doing. Cary turned her attention back to the witch.

What was she doing?

Under her breath, Angie mumbled something in Latin—Cary only recognized it was Latin because she'd taken a semester in college to satisfy her language requirement. She really did suck at languages, but with Latin you didn't actually have to carry on a conversation.

Unfortunately, her Latin was so rusty that recognizing the language was about as good as she could do. She caught a few words she thought she might know, but having learned it written and not spoken, deciphering what Angie was saying was impossible.

After some extended mumbling and a hand gesture that seemed to involve a lot of finger twisting, Angie cursed. "Well, that's not going to work. Let's try…"

She switched languages. French? Maybe Italian or Spanish? Cary wasn't sure, but one of those languages anyway. Angie's hand gestures were harder and briefer now. And very precise. Not the twisting and flow of the earlier movements but distinct, each action having a start and stop before the next gesture started.

Cary found herself just as fascinated watching Angie work as Suzy seemed to be. After another few moments, Angie sighed and dropped her hands to her hips, scowling at the shifter. He'd fallen quiet but his eyes still glowed blue.

"Well shit," Angie said. "The bitch is tricky."

"Which bitch?" Cary and Suzy asked at the same time. The shifter snarled.

"The witch who cursed him," Angie said matter-of-factly. "And she didn't just use a single…school of spell, if you will. She mixed at least two together. Breaking the curse this way is going to take too long."

"Wait, how do you know the witch is a she?" Cary asked.

"How else can you break the curse?" Suzy asked.

"'She' because her…essence I guess you could call it is mixed into the spell. Also some of her blood. Which means when we're done here I can trace her. My alternate plan for breaking the spell is brute force."

"Huh?" Cary said.

"What?" Suzy said.

"No," the shifter growled.

"Don't worry," Angie said to the shifter. "This won't hurt you. The magic will backlash on her. And I'm going to have a hell of a headache later." She stepped close enough to touch the young man.

Cary edged closer too. "You sure touching him is a good idea? Remember, still dangerous?"

"It's the only way. It'll take me ages to unravel the spell itself."

"Just… If he reaches for your throat, I'm going to pull you free."

"Fair enough. I'd appreciate not having my throat ripped out tonight. Hell of a mess."

Cary snorted at the understatement. Suzy gripped Cary's shoulders, leaning into her now so she could better watch what Angie was doing.

"This is all not scientifically possible," Suzy murmured to Cary. "But... But it's happening. The physics must be..." She trailed off as Angie cupped the shifter's cheeks.

"Sorry this is happening to you," Angie said. "But if you'll just hold still and try *not* to attack me, I think I can make it end."

The man nodded, his movement jerky. He flexed his fists over and over but kept his arms at his sides.

Angie smiled at him. He blinked and his mouth dropped open a little. Cary rolled her eyes. Yes, Angie was beautiful. Get over it kid. You've got bigger problems.

In the next moment, Cary realized Angie had used the young man's distraction—maybe even done that to him on purpose—to do...whatever it was she was doing. The hairs on Cary's arms and neck stood on end, like a surge of electricity rose on the air. Tingles raced over her own body, making her shiver with the tickling sensation. She'd felt that sensation once when she was protecting another charge from a wizard's energy blast. It was the feeling of magic. A lot of magic.

Strong magic.

In a voice that sounded significantly deeper than her voice to this point, Angie said something in a language that actually made Cary's ears hurt. It didn't sound like any language spoken on Earth by humans. The resonance of it traveled into her bones.

Damn. Angie was a seriously powerful witch.

Her voice deepened and her words rolled out like thunder. The power seemed to make the ground shake and Cary had to brace herself against the sway. Suzy's hands on her shoulders tightened. Then a noise like something cracking rent the air.

And the shifter sagged to the ground, trembling hard, his body covered in sweat that made his cloth look like he'd just walked through a sudden down pour.

Almost as soon as she'd had the thought, it started to rain.

4

_C_ary glanced up at the soft, wet patter falling on her cheeks and sighed.

"Sorry about that," Angie said, gesturing at the rain. "Side effect of breaking magic with brute force—the way I do it anyway. Tends to shake up the local weather system."

"No problem," Cary said with a shrug.

"When _you_ use brute force on magic, it won't do this," Angie said, holding a hand up to the rain. "You'll just send a backlash through the magical community. They'll feel it, but it won't mess with the mundane world."

"Wait, I can break magic?" Cary asked, wiping rain from her face.

Angie smiled again. "Of course. But Jaxer said you're new to this? Don't worry, you'll pick up all the tricks."

"Cool." She hoped. She glanced at the shifter. "He okay now?"

"He will be when he catches his breath," Angie said.

"Any sense of _why_ a witch would curse him to attack Suzy?" Cary asked.

"We don't really even know each other," Suzy said. "And I don't know any witches. That I'm aware of." She frowned. "Well, there is that woman who comes into my uncle's grocery store. But she's just crazy."

"You know anything about her besides being crazy?" Cary asked. "Does she have a beef with your uncle?"

"Have you spoken to her, given her your name?" Angie asked. "Did she get close enough to get something personal from you, like a strand of hair?"

"Her name is Margarete," the young man said, his voice harsh and gravely. "And she is a little crazy." He glanced up. The blue glow in his eyes was gone, leaving behind a perfectly normal, attractive brown. "But she's also a very powerful bruja."

"That's what that was." Angie groaned and made a face. "She was using an old school Brujaria hex blended with some Cajun magic to complicate things, wasn't she? Maybe even a layer of Santeria? Damn, I should have spotted that. Felt the Spanish and French influences but they were so blended. Missed the West African part..." She trailed off, scowling at nothing as she thought.

After a silent moment, with everyone staring at Angie, Cary finally said, "So...what now? He's okay? Suzy is okay? We all go our separate ways?"

Angie blinked. "Sorry. Still trying to parse out what the bruja did. She's really powerful, blending more than just her own magic to do this curse." Angie glanced at the shifter. "You know of her so the curse was for you? For something you did to her. Or was it specifically focused on Suzy?"

"Me," the young man said. "I refused her. She cursed me to kill..." He glanced away and shrugged. "I see Suzy when she comes into her uncle's store, when I'm working. She doesn't pay any attention to me, but... The bruja took offense when I refused her, and she noticed my attraction to Suzy."

"How old are you?" Cary asked.

"Eighteen."

"Well shit," Cary said. Angie nodded in agreement. "You're just a kid. What the hell?" He looked a little older than eighteen physically but without the crazy blue glow, Cary could definitely see how young he was now.

Suzy peeked at him around Cary's shoulder. "What's your name?" she asked quietly.

"Marco."

"Why haven't you ever said anything to me before?" Suzy asked.

He shrugged and glanced down. "You were always very busy. I didn't want to bother you."

Cary pressed her lips together so she wouldn't grin. This was about the cutest thing she'd ever witnessed. Now that Marco wasn't trying to rip Suzy's throat out of course.

"While this is all adorable," she said aloud, a comment which made both Marco and Suzy blush, "I think we need to do something about this Margarete person so she doesn't keep cursing Marco."

"Fair point," Angie said. "Any idea where she lives, Marco?"

"No."

"But probably the area near my uncle's store, right?" Suzy said. "I mean, why else would she go there? It's just an ordinary grocery store, not a specialty store or anything."

"Very logical. Good point," Cary said. "You will make a brilliant physicist."

"Doctor," Suzy said with a sigh.

"Physicist," Cary said pointedly.

Suzy smiled.

The rain had trickled down to a mist, still wet but less insistent. Cary put her hands on her hips and looked around. "Okay, I think I'd better make sure Suzy gets home safely. Her parents are going to start worrying about her being late."

"Marco, you'll be safe for the rest of the night," Angie said, "but you might want to put some distance between yourself and Suzy. Margarete is probably hurting from the backlash of me breaking her curse, but as soon as she recovers, she might try to do this again."

"You mean I need to leave Portland for good?" he asked, sounding his age now. Very young.

Cary's heart broke.

"No," Angie said. "Just stay away from Suzy for a few days until I can find Margarete and…talk some sense into her."

"She's crazy," Marco insisted. "You won't be able to convince her not to curse me again."

"Oh, I'm sure we can sort it out," Angie said, patting him on the shoulder. Her tone and body language were very maternal now, comforting and confident.

Cary watched in awe as Marco relaxed a bit and nodded.

To Cary, Angie said, "I can trace her through her blood link to the magic, but I'm going to need your help. She's strong enough that it'll be safer if I face her from behind a Protector."

"Oh. Well, sure. Of course. After we get Suzy home?"

"Good."

"Wait, when can I go back to work?" Marco asked. "When will I know it's safe?"

"I could call you?" Suzy suggested shyly.

Cary glanced at her. That was a very clever way to get Marco's phone number. "I can leave a message with Suzy and she can pass it on to you, if that's okay?" she said, glancing in feigned innocence between the two teenagers.

"Yeah, that would be good," Marco said, a little too eagerly.

Cary grinned at Angie over Suzy's head as the girl pulled out her cellphone and took Marco's number.

"All set?" Cary asked. "Good. Now, Marco, you need to leave first so we know Suzy is safe." He turned abruptly to leave, but she raised a hand to stop him. "First, just… Cause I'm still learning. What kind of shifter are you? Exactly?"

"Jaguar," he said. He glanced at Suzy, as if gaging her reaction to that.

"That's really fascinating," Suzy said.

Marco preened.

Cary rolled her eyes. "All right, Romeo, get out of here. Stay away until Suzy calls you."

He nodded, smiled at Suzy, then disappeared into the night, moving at those blinding shifter speeds that left Cary blinking.

"Okay," she said, shaking her head a bit. "Now for you, Suzy." She glanced at Angie. "Then you and me and a visit with a witch?"

Angie grinned. "This should be fun."

"Right," Cary said. "Fun."

5

"*Y*ou sure this is the place?" Cary asked.

She stared up dubiously at the…mansion was probably the word. Although that seemed a pretty tame word for the concoction before them.

"This is the place," Angie said, also staring up at the blended architecture. "At least, this is where the blood signature in the spell led when I scryed."

Cary had been fascinated by the scrying. After they'd dropped Suzy safely home, they'd returned to Angie's car, and the scene of the attack. Angie had opened her trunk, arranged a purple chunk of velvet clothe under an ordinary looking wooden bowl, poured some water into the bowl, and set up a local area map next to it.

Cary had expected some complicated spell or ritual. A lot of very serious "magic" to go into a scrying spell. She'd been utterly amazed at the simplicity of it all. Angie had closed her eyes, taken a few deep breaths, and then focused on the surface of the water. She mumbled a simple spell very quietly, which Cary didn't fully hear—something about blood to owner or something—stirred the surface of the water with her first finger on her right hand, and stared at the water until the surface was still again. Cary waited for some flash of light, an image to show up in the water, something very paranormal. After four months of working with Jaxer, she wouldn't have been surprised by any of that.

What did surprise her was that she didn't see anything at all. Just swirling water coming to a stop in a perfectly ordinary wooden bowl.

Thirty seconds after the water stilled, Angie looked at the map and ran her finger over it. "Here," she said. "Margarete is here."

Here was a mansion hidden at the back of a cul-de-sac behind a thick collection of trees not five blocks from Suzy's uncle's grocery store.

The place was monstrous for the neighborhood and surrounded by more land than any of the other homes in the area. In fact, the rest of the neighborhood was filled with one and two story craftsman family houses, very ordinary stuff for this part of town.

This house was anything but ordinary. The main part was three stories of wood, and stone, and some brick thrown in for good measure. One section looked to be Victorian architecture, another section reminded Cary of a gothic cathedral, still another was very homestead ranch house.

None of it made any real sense and just looking at it made Cary's head hurt. She blinked a few times, trying to bring it all together into a coherent focus. And when she couldn't, she gave up trying.

"Boy that's ugly," Angie said, shaking her head. "Whoever built this place really needed to learn to edit their vision."

Cary snorted. "You think there *was* a vision involved?"

"No. But a woman can hope."

Cary gave her a smile. "So what now?" she asked.

Angie shrugged. "I guess we should go knock on the door. Ring the bell."

"You guess? You don't know?"

"Haven't had to confront a practitioner of Brujaria for evil curses in years. Most modern day brujas and brujos are just reclaiming their culture. They aren't the evil witches passing out destructive hexes of lore. In fact, my first mentor in magic was a bruja. She was brilliant. So knowledgeable." Angie glanced at Cary. "Witches in all cultures and from all disciplines get a bad rap. Sometimes it's earned. Mostly, it's like everything else in life. You get good people and you get bad people."

"You're a good people I take it? Since you work with Jaxer?"

She laughed, a pleasant, deep sound in the chilly night. "I sure hope so—the part about being good that is. I don't exactly work with Jaxer, though. We've crossed paths in the past, so when he needs help with witchy work he tends to tap me. If I'm free, I try to do what I can. I have my own business, though. Psychic readings mostly." She swished her skirt. "I was in the middle of a reading when he called on me tonight. That's why the outfit. It's not really my style. But I find my clients expect a psychic to be a little more colorful and eccentric. They trust my readings more when I dress like this." She shrugged. "And they pay better."

"Yeah, getting paid is definitely good." Cary put her hands on her hips. "So... We knock. The witch comes out. And we just ask her to stop cursing Marco?"

"Sure. We'll try that first."

Cary glanced at Angie as she walked toward the weird mansion's front door—a thick oak thing with iron bolts that looked better suited to a medieval castle. "First?"

"Just keep her from throwing anything ugly at me, and we should be good."

"What if she curses me?"

"That will leave me vulnerable to her spells, so your Protector powers should keep you impervious to her magic while you're keeping me safe."

"You seem to know as much about my magic as I do. Maybe more."

The fact that Angie *knew* about Protectors in the first place was a little surprising. Just as Cary was encouraged to keep the nature of her powers secret, Jaxer apparently kept them secret from all his acquaintances in the supernatural world as well. For her sake. The less people knew about what she was and what she could—and couldn't—do, the safer she was. Angie was the first person Cary had encountered outside

Jaxer and the Nags that not only knew what Protectors were but also knew how the defensive magic worked.

Angie waved away Cary's vague concern as they reached the wooden castle door. "I learned about Protectors years ago, before meeting Jaxer. Don't worry, he's not giving away your secrets."

"You keep saying 'years' like you're a lot older than you are," Cary commented.

Angie looked in her late twenties, maybe early thirties. Closer to Cary's age anyway. But at almost twenty-seven, Cary didn't feel she could say things like "years ago" and still mean a time period when she'd been an adult. Years ago could mean the years when she was in college. Maybe. The way Angie said it, though, it sounded…longer.

To be fair, no one knew how old Cary was most of the time either. Guesses tended to range from twenty up to the mid-thirties. And thanks to this Protector gig, her biological aging process had apparently slowed down—bonus! Still, Angie couldn't be all that old.

"Probably because I've had a very interesting life," Angie said matter-of-factly.

"You can't be more than, what, thirty?" Cary guessed. "How much could you have fit in in only thirty years?"

Angie grinned. "If we get out of this situation without getting cursed or killed, we can sit down with a bottle of Tequila and I will tell all." She shrugged. "Well some. Some of it isn't mine to tell."

"Huh?"

"Later. I promise." Angie knocked on the wooden door.

Inside, Cary heard the sound reverberate and echo. The entryway must be bigger than it looked.

Almost as soon as the sound stopped, Cary felt a tingling along her skin, a warning signal she was starting to heed. She stepped in front of Angie, just enough to keep her safe from whatever came out of that door.

"Thanks," Angie said. "I *think* my warding charm would have held off that attack, but I'm not sure."

"Attack?" Cary blinked over her shoulder. "We just got attacked?"

"I did. The spell was designed specifically for other witches."

"Whoa. Scary. You didn't get hurt?"

"No, no. I'm fine." She tilted her head to one side. "I can't really sense when a Protector is channeling their powers—your bosses' magic is really really different from anything I've ever worked with. As far as I can tell, it's completely different from any other kinds of magic in the world. But with you, I can kind of sense…" She shrugged and let out a half-laugh. "Well, I sense power. It's kind of like an undercurrent of *you*. If you know what I mean."

"Not a clue," Cary said. "I was as ordinary as they come before the Nags tricked me into this job."

"Tricked you?"

"Long story. But I don't have any innate powers beyond what they gave me. And according to Jaxer, those don't even work when I'm not protecting someone."

"Maybe it's just the way you channel the magic, then," Angie said with a shrug.

Cary started to ask more, but before she could, the huge oak door swung open.

6

<hr>

Neither Cary nor Angie moved into the empty entryway beyond the oak door. It was high-ceilinged and matched the front door, having a vaguely castle look to it. Stone walls with hung tapestries, a dark wooden bench to one side, and two metal rings hanging from the ceiling with light bulbs that mimicked flickering candlelight circling them.

Cary frowned up at the…chandeliers she supposed they'd be called, just to make sure those weren't real candles. That seemed like a fire hazard. But nope, just ordinary light bulbs giving off a very effective illusion.

The air was scented with some sort of herb Cary couldn't identify. It reminded her of the meditation school she'd gone to exactly once in college so she thought maybe patchouli or sandalwood. Whatever it was, it was strong, tickling at her nose. She pressed her tongue to the roof of her mouth to keep from sneezing.

The tingling along her skin intensified with each moment they stood there. She wanted to shake off the sensation. It was creepy, like bugs crawling over her skin. But she'd already learned in the last three months that nothing she did helped. She'd just have to deal with the buggy sensation.

"Whatever she's got coming out that door is strong," Cary commented.

"Yup," Angie agreed. "I'm very glad you're here."

"Thanks. Me too." Glad she could keep Angie safe anyway.

A misting rain began as they continued to wait, the tricky kind of rain that soaked through clothes even though she could barely feel it. Cary didn't risk taking her eyes off the open doorway and the empty space beyond, but she did swipe a hand over her face to keep the water out of her eyes. Despite the new rip in her coat from Marco's attack, she was grateful the thick wool still kept out the damp chill.

The silence and the tingling continued for long moments. Cary's patience was stretched thin. She'd never been very good at waiting. She was that kid who always gave herself away during hide-and-seek. It took a great deal of willpower not to fidget.

Finally, after what felt like twenty minutes of just standing there, a woman emerged from the gloom at the far end of the entryway. Her entrance was very dramatic, as she seemed to materialize out of the black hole that was another doorway and stroll forward under the flickering imitation candlelight.

Cary scowled and shook her head. "You don't think all this is a little over the top?" she said to the witch as she approached. "I mean, really, a castle?"

The woman smiled, flashing too-white teeth. She was stunningly gorgeous, with thick, smooth black hair, dark eyes, perfect skin, flawless makeup, and beautiful red lips. She was curvy and wore a form fitting white dress to emphasize those curves. Her spiky high heels made her muscled calves look spectacular.

But Cary noticed she was significantly older than teenage Marco. Well-kept, but definitely closer to fifty than twenty.

Hitting on a teenager. What was this lady thinking? The kid was only barely legal. And then getting in a tiff and cursing him just because he said no? That was just rude.

"You have strong magic, witch," Margarete said. To Cary. She only flicked a passing glance at Angie, her full attention on Cary.

Cary raised her brows. "Not a witch." She nodded back to Angie. "She's got that covered."

The bruja looked more fully at Angie. "You broke my curse? That wasn't very nice of you."

"Wasn't a very nice curse," Angie said.

Her voice had deepened a bit, taking on the same kind of resonance Cary had heard in it while she'd been trying to untangle Margarete's spell.

"And really you need to stop hitting on teenagers," Cary added. "You're too old for him."

Margarete's eyes narrowed to slits. "Dangerous words. Tempting my anger is stupid."

Cary shrugged. "You might want to get some help with that. An anger management class maybe."

Margarete snarled. "Your magic won't protect you from my curses, bitch. I am too powerful."

"I'm sure you are," Cary said. "I saw what you did to poor Marco."

That earned Cary a vicious smile. "No one denies me what I want."

"Yeah, well, we're going to do just that because what you want is wrong, and sending that kid to *kill* the girl he has a crush on was beyond mean. You need to leave them alone."

"Or what?" she snapped. "What do you think you can do to me?"

"I can get between you and anyone you want to curse and keep them safe," Cary said. "But really, I'm not the one you should be worried about."

Margarete flipped her hair and settled her hands on her hips. The whole gesture was sexy and confident and perfectly executed. If she wasn't such an evil bitch, Cary might have been impressed.

"I'm not worried about anyone." She gestured with one immaculately manicured hand to the house behind her. "All this… Bought by the money powerful people pay me for my spells. I curse their enemies, heal their illnesses, give them charms to make them wealthier. In exchange, they give me everything I want."

She leaned a little closer, and Cary caught a whiff of a delicious perfume. Probably something expensive, Cary guessed with no little internal eye-rolling.

"My powers are immense," Margarete said. "Crossing me, displeasing me is dangerous. And you have displeased me by coming here."

Cary grinned. "Yeah, I've noticed that. Bet you don't get a lot of Jehovah's Witnesses stopping by, do you?"

"You're very arrogant. And very stupid."

"You keep telling me that, and yet here I am, standing in your doorway. Not taking any damage at all from all that magic you keep throwing at us. Maybe I'm not the stupid one?"

Margarete said something under her breath, hissing out the words in Spanish if Cary had to make a guess. Nothing she could understand, but the words were delivered with a vicious twist of the woman's mouth. She pulled a bag from behind her—Cary hadn't even noticed it —opened the small leather satchel and threw its contents in Cary's direction.

Cary watched the particles of the white powder float in the air in front of her, dancing like dust in sunlight. Thanks to the fineness of the powder, she could almost see the edges of her shield a few feet in front of her, a clear and distinct line between her and Margarete.

Actually getting to see her magic, magic she couldn't even sense, made her smile. That was pretty cool.

Margarete's words turned into a string of obscenities. Not the kind of cursing she'd intended with the powder, Cary assumed.

Cary waited her out, smiling patiently until she stopped cussing. She was aware of Angie murmuring almost soundlessly behind her, and she could faintly sense Angie's hands moving near her back, using Cary to hide those movements.

When Margarete finally stopped ranting, she was breathing heavy, some of her elegant smoothness gone now, her anger making her eyes glimmer with a wild, crazed light. "Whatever you are," she said, her voice low and harsh, "I will destroy you for your interference. You will suffer untold horrors, wishing for death that will never come."

"Scary," Cary said pleasantly. "No. But it was a good effort at trying to scare me."

"You are not impervious, bitch. I will make you suffer, make everyone you've ever known, everyone you've ever loved suffer. I will slowly kill this witch you're trying to shield, making you watch as I cut out her beating heart. Then I will go after your family. And you will watch them cry out in pain."

"You realize you're just making things harder on yourself with all that, right," Cary said. Margarete's intent to hurt others, especially threatening Angie, kept Cary's powers working. In her anger, she was ensuring Cary could hold her off.

Cary wasn't going to explain that to her in any kind of detail, of course.

"So," Cary said, "what I need you to do is stop throwing around curses, and leave Marco and Suzy alone. They're just kids and you're a grown ass woman who should know better than to hit on teenagers. In fact, cursing that kid just because he doesn't want you shows a level of insecurity on your part that I'd think would embarrass you."

"I am so going to enjoy cutting you into little pieces," Margarete purred.

Cary sighed. "Yeah, that's not going to happen. And really, you need to stop. Get some therapy. You obviously have issues. Therapy can help."

Margarete's outraged scream made Cary wince. She'd managed to whip the witch into such a state of anger, she actually threw herself at Cary, attempting to physically attack her. The move only got her tossed backward into her castle hallway.

Cary shook her head. "Stop already. You're being unreasonable."

Margarete threw herself at Cary again, this time holding a wicked looking knife in one hand. Damn. Cary hadn't even seen where the knife had come from. If she weren't so certain her powers were working, she might have been a little nervous.

Probably more than a little. Margarete was scary as all hell. Cary was pretty pleased she kept threatening other people so the Protector magic kept working.

Margarete slashed at her with the knife, never able to get close enough to hurt Cary, but the anger and strength in her attack was impressive.

Cary might have gone a little too far in taunting the woman.

But Angie had needed the time.

In a voice so deep it made the hairs on Cary's arms stand up, Angie said, "What you have rot comes back in earnest. Threefold returns that which you've furnished."

Cary raised her brows at the weird rhyme and glanced back. Angie's face was set, her brow furrowed in concentration. Her hands wove a pattern in the air now, sketching a series of shapes that seemed to leave blue light lingering so that Cary could almost see forms. And then she flared her hands wide, throwing those shapes at Margarete. The power in the spell rolled past Cary, a wave of energy she felt indirectly.

A clap of thunder made her jump.

Margarete screamed, this time in denial. "You can't," she said. "I am protected. You can't."

Even as she spoke, she started batting at the air like she was being attacked by bugs. Cary's eyes widened as welts rose on the woman's perfect skin, and blood dripped from a wound Cary couldn't see, staining the white dress red. Ew.

Margarete's scream turned to one of pain, a sound so horrible Cary wanted to cover her ears. The woman stumbled back into her home, thrashing and batting at an invisible attacker. The heavy wooden door slammed in Cary's face with a loud echo that abruptly cut off the torturous screams from within.

"Uhm," she said after a quiet moment. "That was bad."

She faced Angie. Angie shrugged.

"What did you do?" Cary asked.

"Turned her magic back on her," Angie said. She headed down the stone walk toward the street.

Cary glanced at the oak door, hesitating only a moment before she followed Angie.

"So...," Cary said. "So all that was stuff she'd done to other people?"

"Yup."

"And you didn't actually cause any of the…"

"The icky stuff?" Angie shook her head. "Nope. If she'd only provided good magic charms to her clients, that's all she'd have gotten back. My spell was pretty agnostic that way. Just an old school, whatever-you-put-out-you-get-back kind of thing. She had a ward against bounce-back spells, so I had to work my way through that first. Thanks for distracting and stalling her. That was really helpful."

"Uh huh." Cary glanced over her shoulder at the house. "What will happen to her?"

"Depends on what she's done. But I don't think you'll have any more trouble from her. If she survives her own curses, she won't want to send out anymore evil spells. They'll just return to her threefold. And after tonight… Even a crazy woman wouldn't want to suffer that."

"How long will your spell last? Can she break it?"

"Not now."

"Uhm…" Cary paused. "How?"

Angie grinned. "Kind of complicated to explain. Why don't we get that Tequila and we can have a long chat."

"Yeah, I could use a Tequila shot about now." She looked at Margarete's weird house again. "Maybe three."

Angie laughed. "And food. I'm starving after all that. I've got all the fixings for nachos back at my place. What do you say?"

"I love nachos," Cary said. "But I need to swing by my house first and let my dog out."

"Oh, what kind of dog do you have?"

They started walking back to Angie's car again.

"A Labrador puppy." She thought it best not to mention Buck's actual nature. At least not yet. Though, she had a feeling she could tell Angie, and Angie would understand.

"I love dogs," Angie said.

"I thought witches preferred cats."

"Some do. I'm more of a dog person. And owls. I love owls."

"Me too!"

As Angie climbed into the driver's side of her car, Cary glanced one last time at Margarete's house. Then she slipped into her seat.

"So do you think Marco and Suzy will get together?" she asked as she buckled her seatbelt.

"That would be really cute." Angie started the car. "Do you think she'll be okay with him being a jaguar shifter?"

"If he's okay with her being a physicist."

The misty rain opened up, turning into a downpour. As they passed Margarete's home, Cary shivered a little. Yeah, she needed that Tequila now.

And nachos. This night had definitely earned her some nachos.

WHEN CARY MET LUCY

In Cary Redmond's life as a Protector, magic does not always cause the mayhem…

Running into the darkness under a bridge is not the sort of thing an ordinary woman should do late at night. But for Cary Redmond, it's just part of her job as a magical Protector. And frankly, after the not-so-fun dinner with her parents, charging into danger to rescue the innocent seems like a good idea. Almost as good as the donut she was going to have before her Protector senses went off.

What she discovers in those midnight shadows, however, changes her perspective completely on women running into the darkness under a bridge. And sets the stage for a brand new friendship.

1

———————

*C*ary Redmond's Protector instincts kicked in when she was on her way to Voodoo Donuts after a less-than-fun dinner with her parents. The urge to keep moving, to get somewhere fast was strong enough to get her past the smell of fried pastry. Which meant it was a pretty strong imperative.

Someone was in danger and it was now her job to help. She even got paid for it. After a year and a half, and still not entirely sure how she'd ended up in this job, she had to admit, getting *paid* to do it really helped.

The tingling along her shoulders urged her toward the river and the Burnside Bridge. She didn't usually walk along the Willamette this late at night, and she wouldn't normally go alone to the Burnside Bridge— the homeless that camped there could be unpredictable—but the closer she got, the harder her instincts pushed her. The tingles a long her shoulders and rolling down her spine were like ants on her skin. She couldn't have turned back if she'd wanted to. Though, in all honesty, she didn't usually *want* to turn back when someone needed her help.

Most of the time.

So long as it wasn't one of her mentor Jaxer's "missions," which usually had nothing to do with her actual job that she got paid for, but invariably got her into a lot of trouble.

The night was dark and warm, the breeze off the river cooling, though not really what she might call refreshing. The stench from under the Bridge carried on the wind, the weight of unwashed human bodies and piss strong the closer she got. She wrinkled her nose and squinted into the gloom under the bridge, trying to pinpoint the source of all her growing anxiety.

Her heart hammered hard and she had to work to control her breathing. Until she was actually protecting someone, she was as vulnerable to muggings, and worse, as any other mundane person. She had to suppress a screech when a hunched, scraggly-bearded homeless man came charging out of the dark, right into her face, hollering about crazy women. At first, she thought he was talking about her, but he moved past her, glaring over his shoulder, continuing to curse the crazy woman before moving on to a rant about a government conspiracy. At least, she thought that was what the last part was about. He was moving fast away from the bridge so it was hard to tell.

Her heart broke a little for him—he needed somewhere safe to be, not living under a bridge—but then the sounds of more approaching footsteps distracted her. Half a dozen more homeless people hurried past her, reminding her of people fleeing a disaster. She swallowed hard.

What the hell was going on under that bridge?

She was a little desperate to find someone to protect now. The magic the Nags—her North American Fae bosses—had given her only activated when she was putting herself between good guys and bad guys, and once she was there, she was a Kevlar vest of protection. But until then, she was a vulnerable sack of bones. And really, she didn't want to get mugged tonight. Or worse.

She swallowed hard, her pulse thumping in her throat, her palms starting to sweat as she got deeper into the darkness under the bridge, closer to the river. Concrete pillars over a damp concrete ground looked like pale sentinels in the dark. She squinted at the chainlink fence surrounding some construction equipment near the river. She couldn't see anything happening there. Beyond that were the low pillars and fencing lining the river walk, and beyond that the river itself. But she still couldn't see anyone.

Where the hell was the someone in trouble?

Then she heard it. A sound like a grunt. A high female voice saying something sharp. Another very male shout. Some male laughter. And the distinctive sound of a body hitting the ground with a loud thump.

Cary took off at a run, charging toward the noise. She wasn't a natural runner. Running really wasn't a part of her nature. But when she was racing to protect someone, she could run like...well, a much faster human than she was normally.

She skidded to a halt at the back of the fenced in construction equipment, just at the edge of the water. Thanks to her powers, she could see the scene clearly now. But what she saw took a few minutes to register.

A girl that was *maybe* five foot tall, with curly red hair pulled into a tight bun and wearing jeans and a loose t-shirt over a petite frame, stood surrounded by three very large men. Cary made a move to reach her but before she could take a step, one of the men charged the girl, the girl shifted her weight, and the man went flying into the chainlink fence with a resounding crash.

The girl had tossed a man twice her size easily. With barely a sound.

The other two men charged the girl at the same time. In movements so subtle they didn't actually look like much, the girl stepped first one way, then the other, her arms moving in graceful arcs as she seemed to effortlessly toss the attackers one way and the other. One man hit the ground with a thud, the other flipped head over ass onto the ground at the girl's feet. He cursed and tried to stand, but she flipped him onto his stomach and retched his arm up and back, wrapping her own around his extended limb, bringing it close to her body in what looked like an embrace, and twisting. The movement looked gentle. The man's scream of pain was not.

Cary blinked a few times, squinting at the scene. Not sure she was seeing this right.

The girl moved like a human, not at the supernatural speeds of say a shapeshifter or a vampire. But she didn't seem to be putting much effort into hurting men that were significantly bigger than her.

The guy she'd thrown into the chainlink charged her again. Cary stepped forward to help, but paused when the girl ducked under the new attack, rose up gracefully with her hands on the man's shoulder and waist, and tossed him toward the fence lining the river. He flew high enough he almost dropped over the barrier and had to scramble back across the metal brackets to dry land.

The third man flew at the girl. She rolled out of his way, and popped up onto her feet as he spun to charge her again. She squatted low, once again braced her hands on the man's shoulder and stomach, then lifted up and tossed him over her head so he landed with a bone-jarring, breath-steeling splat on the hard ground.

Cary actually winced with that hit.

She watched in stupefied awe. If she was here to protect that girl, the girl didn't need protecting. Cary was pretty sure she'd dislocated the one guy's shoulder. The other two were limping as they attacked her again—only to be tossed onto their asses. Again.

The first homeless man's muttered curses about crazy women came back to Cary and she wondered if she was here to protect the men getting tossed around. That didn't seem right. They were attacking a little girl half their size. If they needed Cary's protection, they'd be trying to get away from the girl. Wouldn't they?

But they kept going after her. Cary didn't protect bad guys who were trying to hurt other people. She protected the people they were trying to hurt.

Huh.

Putting her hands on her hips, she watched the fight, trying to decide why the hell her powers had led her here. This girl, whoever she was, needed no help at all.

Then Cary saw the flicker of light on a long, sharp blade. The man holding the knife had just been thrown against the river railing and the girl was occupied with the other two attackers—the guy with the dislocated shoulder really should have called it quits.

Cary took two steps toward the fight, then watched in amazement as the girl shifted her stance, grabbed the man with the knife by his wrist, pulled his arm straight and drove her hand up into his elbow. The man's elbow bent in a very unnatural way, and Cary heard the snap of bone from several yards away.

The man screamed, loud and unexpectedly high, and dropped the knife in a clatter.

So much for the knife being a threat.

But the other two men seemed to lose their minds at the actual bone break their comrade had suffered. They charged the girl at once. Given their own injuries, given what that little girl was doing to them, they really really should have just stopped.

This whole thing was getting out of hand. Cary worked her way closer, trying not to distract the girl, but determined to get between the men and the girl so she could put an end to the fight. The men were gonna end up in pieces soon if they didn't stop.

From the corner of her eye, and with an instinct she'd only developed since becoming a Protector, Cary spotted the movement of shadows near one of the pale concrete pillars. Some faint sound, like a click, reached her despite the shouts and curses from the fight. She had just enough time to glance in the direction of the moving shadow, just enough time to see the flash of light, and she was moving—this time at speeds most humans couldn't.

She got between the girl and the bullet just as the sound of the gun's retort broke through the night air.

2

The clink clink of metal dropping onto concrete was the only sound in the otherwise sudden silence. Everyone froze in place, even the man with the gun.

Cary pressed a hand to her ribs where the bullet had hit her, crunched into a flattened and harmless lump, and then dropped away.

Ow. She hated getting shot.

The bruising would be significant later, she thought with a sigh. And she really didn't want to go to the hospital and try to explain the pinpoint crack in her rib. Again. It was getting harder and harder to explain these weird injuries she sometimes got when she had to jump between an attacker and an attackee. The wound would heal pretty quickly—another perk of her job. Maybe she could get away with *not* going to the hospital this time.

She glanced behind her. The little girl's dark brown eyes were wide in her pale face. But this close, Cary realized the "girl" was actually an adult woman.

"You okay?" she asked the woman.

"Are you?" the woman asked.

She had the cutest, high-pitched voice Cary had ever heard. She not only looked like a little girl, she sounded like one too. Geez, no wonder she'd learned how to toss around men twice her size.

"I'm fine," Cary said.

"You just got shot," the woman pointed out.

"Na, he missed." She waved away the incident as if it was nothing and stepped on the smushed bullet in an attempt to hide it.

She technically wasn't supposed to tell people what she did. It was for her own safety as well as theirs. Because of the way her powers worked, if someone knew what she was, they could easily kill her by simply trying to kill *her* and not meaning any harm to anyone else near her. If bad guys meant harm to anyone around her, though, even if they also wanted to hurt Cary, Cary's powers would work and she'd be as safe as her charges. The Protector magic was purely defensive, and it was designed to work *through* her, not *for* her.

Her powers required a tricky balance of intentions on the bad guys' part, a balance that was more easily maintained when no one actually knew what she was. If they didn't know she was a Protector or what a Protector's vulnerabilities were, Cary was significantly less likely to get killed.

Which was a good thing.

The man with the gun lifted his arm to fire again, but Cary raised a hand, palm out to stop him. Since everything that had been happening in the last few minutes was so strange, the man actually stopped without shooting her again.

"Look," she said in what she hoped was a very reasonable tone, "I've already called the cops. The woman has thoroughly kicked your asses, which you'll have to explain to the police, and if you get caught mugging us with a gun, the punishment is a lot worse."

At least she thought it might be. She was bluffing in a big way. It hadn't even occurred to her to call the cops. She tried to avoid them because she didn't want to have to explain to authority figures how she got shot without actually getting hurt beyond some bruising and a cracked rib.

She waved her cellphone at the surrounding men, to make it seem like she'd actually used it, and all four of them took a few steps back.

They exchanged looks silently, then without a word, all four hurried into the darkness beyond the bridge, three of them limping and holding various wounded body parts.

"I hope they actually go to the hospital," Cary muttered. "Some of those injuries are gonna need treatment." She turned to face the woman. "You sure you're okay? Do you need a hospital?"

"Of course not. I'm not the one who was shot."

"I wasn't shot," Cary insisted.

"Sure," the woman said. She glanced down at Cary's foot still covering the smushed bullet.

Cary decided a change of subject was super necessary. "So what was all that about? What were you doing here? Looking for a fight?"

"Of course not," the woman said again, putting her hands on her hips and lifting her chin. "I would never purposefully start a fight. I'm too well trained and could really hurt someone."

"I noticed that. It was a pretty impressive display actually."

"Thanks." The woman grinned. "I've been training since I was two. I should be pretty good at all this by now."

"So… If you weren't looking for a fight, why were you here?"

She shrugged. "I was having a tough day and decided I needed some quiet time at the Japanese memorial. I like the area and the cherry trees and the sounds of the river. It sooths me."

"Fair enough. In the dark?" Since it was summer, the days did last pretty long. But it was well after midnight now.

"I've been sitting under the trees for a while," the woman admitted with an embarrassed wince. "I didn't notice how late it had gotten."

"Ah. That still doesn't explain how you ended up under the bridge."

The woman turned then, hunting for something near the chainlink fence. Cary used her distraction to kick the bullet away into the darker shadows. The woman trotted to the fence, bent to retrieve something, and hurried back with a bag in her hand. Cary heard the little mewing sound of the kitten even before the woman showed her the fuzzy calico baby wrapped in the canvas sack.

"Those assholes were going to toss this precious baby into the river," the woman said in an outraged tone.

Cary gasped. "They were going to drown the kitten? That's horrible. Why? Poor little thing." She held her hand out to the kitten and let it sniff her. When the baby gave her a little lick with its rough tongue, Cary took that as a friending gesture and gave the baby a head scratch.

"I was on my way back to the garage where I parked my car," the woman said, her attention also on the orange and white kitten, "when I heard them talking. One of those assholes was telling the other they had to get rid of the 'stupid cat' first."

"First?"

"I didn't hear what they were planning on doing after they got rid of the cat. And they didn't see fit to explain what the hurry was when I intervened."

"Bastards," Cary said, still scratching the now purring kitten behind its little ears. She grinned at the baby. "How could anyone hurt someone so adorable?"

She worried a bit about what the men had planned *after* casually drowning a cat, but given the injuries they'd all taken, she figured they'd be harmless enough for the rest of the night. After tonight... That would have to be someone else's concern. Though, she might mention this to Jaxer. He could probably just check on the men, maybe alert the authorities to them.

"I can't believe you took on four huge guys just to save a kitten," Cary said to the woman. "That's really impressive."

"What else could I do? Poor little baby needed my help," she murmured to the kitten.

"I ended up in my current job doing something similar," Cary said quietly. "So...what now? Should we take the kitten to a shelter?"

"No," the woman said, almost sounding offended. "She's mine now. I saved her. I'm responsible for her. That's how it works."

Cary raised her eyebrows at that. Did that mean she was responsible for all the people she saved doing her job? That could get out of hand pretty quickly.

"What were you doing here?" the woman asked, distracting her.

"Oh. I…uhm, I was on my way to get a donut after a really painful dinner with my parents, and I heard the sounds of a fight."

"You came to help? That's very sweet. Why was dinner with your parents painful?"

They turned in unison, walking back toward the main road, falling into conversation as if they'd known each other for years.

"Oh, they're just concerned about me," Cary said. "I switched jobs a year and a half ago, and my mother doesn't understand. She keeps pressuring me to go back to the 'safe' career I had planned."

"My fathers do that, too, only with relationships. They want me to move back to Hawaii and marry someone nice and 'secure.'"

"My mother is doing that now too!" Cary said. "Well, not the part about moving to Hawaii." She grinned. "But she is nagging me about finding someone and getting married. Especially since my little sister got married last year. Now all I hear about is how I should be settling down."

"Right? I know they mean well, but really, I have bigger things to worry about right now."

"Exactly. What's your worry?"

"My dojo. It's doing okay, but the landlord wants to raise the rent again, and I'm not making enough to afford the increase. I either need to change locations to someplace cheaper or find a way to bring in more students. My dads just want me to move home, but I don't want to live in Hawaii anymore. I like seasons. If I can't find a way to keep my business open, though, I might have to move. That's what I was sitting out by the river thinking about earlier."

"Ah. That is tricky." Cary gave the woman a side lock. "I think this discussion calls for donuts."

"I couldn't agree more," she said emphatically. "My name's Lucy, by the way. Lucy Evans-Nakada."

"Cary Redmond. It's a pleasure to meet you, Lucy. And if you don't mind my saying, you have the most adorable little voice."

"Thank you. For that crack, you can pay for the donuts."

Cary grinned. "Deal. Now about this dojo of yours, do you think you might be able to teach me some self-defense skills? I think it could be really helpful in my new job." Her magic gave her all the abilities she needed to protect people in the moment, but Cary could see having the *actual* ability to defend herself without magic being very useful.

"Of course I can teach you," Lucy said without hesitation. "I'm an excellent instructor. What exactly *is* your job that you'd need to learn self-defense?"

"Ah," Cary said with a shrug. "That's a much longer story. And definitely requires donuts. And maybe a bottle of wine."

"Cary," Lucy said in her sweet little voice, "I think this is the beginning of a beautiful friendship."

Cary laughed. She couldn't agree more.

Thanks for reading some of the earliest adventures in Cary Redmond's life as a magical Protector. These are some of the most important people (and pets) in Cary's life. All of them travel with her throughout the series and I loved being able to tell the origin stories of these friendships. I hope you enjoyed their stories too.

If this is your first introduction to the Cary Redmond series, don't miss the first book, THE TROUBLE WITH BLACK CATS AND DEMONS, out now!

For more on me and my books, you can join my newsletter (http://eepurl.com/OxQQL), visit my website (https://www.katsimons.-com), or follow my author page at your favorite vendor.

Thanks again for reading!

~Kat

BOOKS BY KAT SIMONS

THE CARY REDMOND SERIES

1 – The Trouble Black Cats and Demons

2 – The Trouble with Ghouls and Serial Killers

3 – The Trouble with Leopard Queens and Shifter Wars

4 – The Trouble with Baby Gods and Vampires

5 – The Trouble with Magic and Faery Curses COMING SOON

CARY REDMOND SHORT STORIES

When Cary Met Jaxer

When Cary Met Pickles

When Cary Met Angie

When Cary Met Lucy

When Cary Met Marianne

Cary and Deacon (Try to) Go On A Date

Date Night Take Two

Third Date's the Charm

Cary vs the Goblin King

Dinner with the Jones

TIGER SHIFTERS SERIES

1 – Once Upon a Tiger

2 – Along Came a Tiger

3 – Here There Be Tigers

4 – Her Tiger To Take

5 – To Tempt a Tiger

6 – Down Will Come Tiger

7 – To Catch a Tiger

8 – What a Tiger Wants

9 – Taming Her Tiger

ABOUT THE AUTHOR

Kat Simons earned her Ph.D. in animal behavior, working with animals as diverse as dolphins and deer. She brought her experience and knowledge of biology to her paranormal romance and urban fantasy fiction, where she delights in taking nature and turning it on its ear. Her Tiger Shifters series combines romance and the otherworldly with heart-pounding action adventure. Her latest urban fantasy romance series follows the adventures of Protector Cary Redmond as she tries to manage her personal life while saving the world. A lot.

For something a little different, Kat also publishes fantasy romance, science fiction romance, and the occasional hockey romance under the name Isabo Kelly (http://www.isabokelly.com).

After traveling the world, Kat now lives in New York City with her family. She is a stay-at-home mom and a full time writer.

For more on Kat and her future books:

Website: https://www.katsimons.com
Newsletter: http://eepurl.com/OxQQL